A Princess of Thule

William Black

BIBLIOLIFE

A PRINCESS OF THULE.

BY

WILLIAM BLACK,

AUTHOR OF "STRANGE ADVENTURES OF A PHAETON," &c. &c.

IN THREE VOLUMES.

VOL. III.

SECOND EDITION.

London:

MACMILLAN AND CO.

1874.

CONTENTS.

CHAPTER VII.

CHAPTER VIII.

CHAPTER IX.

A PRINCESS OF THULE.

CHAPTER I.

A NEW DAY BREAKS.

WAS this, then, the end of the fair and beautiful romance that had sprung up and blossomed so hopefully in the remote and bleak island, amid the silence of the hills and moors and the wild twilights of the north, and set round about, as it were, by the cold sea-winds and the sound of the Atlantic waves? Who could have fancied, looking at those two young folks as they wandered about the shores of the island, as they sailed on the still moonlight nights through the channels of Loch Roag, or as they sang together of an evening in the little parlour of the house at Borvabost, that all the delight and wonder of life then apparently opening out before them was so soon and so suddenly to collapse, leaving them in outer darkness and despair? All their difficulties had been got over. From one side and from another they had received generous help, friendly advice, self-sacrifice to start them on a path that seemed to be strewn with sweet-smelling flowers. And here was the end—a wretched girl, blinded and bewildered, flying from her husband's house and seeking refuge in the great world of London, careless whither she went.

Whose was the fault? Which of them had been mistaken up there in the North, laying the way open for a bitter disappointment? Or had either of them failed to carry out that unwritten contract entered into in the halcyon period of courtship, by which two young people promise to be and remain to each other all that they then appear?

Lavender, at least, had no right to complain. If the real Sheila turned out to be something different to the Sheila of his fancy, he had been abundantly warned that such would be the case. He had even accepted it as probable, and said that as the Sheila whom he might come to know must doubtless be better than the Sheila whom he had imagined, there was little danger in store for either. He would love the true Sheila even better than the creature of his brain. Had he done so? He found beside him this proud and sensitive Highland girl, full of generous impulses that craved for the practical work of helping other people, longing, with the desire of a caged bird, for the free winds and light of heaven, the sight of hills and the sound of seas; and he could not understand why she should not conform to the usages of city life. He was disappointed that she did not do so. The imaginative Sheila, who was to appear as a wonderful Sea-princess in London drawing-rooms, had disappeared now; and the real Sheila, who did not care to go with him into that society which he loved or affected to love, he had not learned to know.

And had she been mistaken in her estimate of Frank Lavender's character? At the very moment of her leaving her husband's house, if she had been asked the question, she would have turned and proudly answered, "No!" She had been disappointed—so grievously disappointed that her heart seemed to be breaking over it; but the manner in which Frank Lavender had fallen away from the promise he had given was due, not to himself, but to the influence of the society around him. Of that she was quite assured. He had shown himself careless, indifferent, inconsiderate to the verge of cruelty;

B 2

but he was not, she had convinced herself, con-
sciously cruel, nor yet selfish, nor radically bad-
hearted in any way.   In her opinion, at least, he
was courageously sincere, to the verge of shocking people who mistook his frankness for impu-
dence.   He was recklessly generous; he would
have given the coat off his back to a beggar, at
the instigation of a sudden impulse, provided he
could have got into a cab before any of his
friends saw him; he had rare abilities, and at
times wildly ambitious dreams, not of his own
glorification, but of what he would do to celebrate the beauty and the graces of the Princess
whom he fancied he had married.   It may seem
hard of belief that this man, judging him by
his actions at this time, could have had anything
of thorough self-forgetfulness and manliness in
his nature.   But when things were at their very
worst—when he appeared to the world as a self-
indulgent idler, careless of a noble woman's un-
bounded love—when his indifference, or worse,
had actually driven from his house a young wife
who had especial claims on his forbearance and
consideration—there were two people who still
believed in Frank Lavender.   They were Sheila
Mackenzie and Edward Ingram; and a man's
wife and his oldest friend generally know something about his real nature, its besetting tempta-

tions, its weakness, its strength, and its possibilities.

Of course Ingram was speedily made aware of
all that had happened. Lavender went home at
the appointed hour to luncheon, accompanied by
his three acquaintances. He had met them ac-
cidentally in the forenoon ; and as Mrs. Lorraine
was most particular in her inquiries about Sheila,
he thought he could not do better than ask her
there and then, with her mother and Lord
Arthur, to have luncheon at two. What followed
on his carrying the announcement to Sheila we
know. He left the house, taking it for granted
that there would be no trouble when he returned.
Perhaps he reproached himself for having spoken
so sharply ; but Sheila was really very thoughtless in such matters. At two o'clock everything
would be right. Sheila must see how it would
be impossible to introduce a young Highland
serving-maid to two fastidious ladies and the
son of a great Conservative peer.

Lavender met his three friends once more and
walked up to the house with them, letting them
in, indeed, with his own latch-key. Passing the
dining-room, he saw that the table was laid there.
This was well. Sheila had been reasonable.

They went upstairs to the drawing-room.
Sheila was not there. Lavender rang the bell,

and bade the servant tell her mistress she was wanted.

"Mrs. Lavender has gone out, sir," said the servant.

"Oh, indeed," he said, taking the matter quite coolly. "When?"

"A quarter of an hour ago, sir. She went out with the—the young lady who came this morning."

"Very well. Let me know when luncheon is ready."

Lavender turned to his guests, feeling a little awkward, but appearing to treat the matter in a light and humorous way. He imagined that Sheila, resenting what he had said, had resolved to take Mairi away, and find her lodgings elsewhere. Perhaps that might be done in time to let Sheila come back to receive his guests.

Sheila did not appear, however, and luncheon was announced.

"I suppose we may as well go down," said Lavender, with a shrug of his shoulders. "It is impossible to say when she may come back. She is such a good-hearted creature that she would never think of herself or her own affairs in looking after this girl from Lewis."

They went down stairs, and took their places at the table.

" For my part," said Mrs. Lorraine, " I think it is very unkind not to wait for poor Mrs. Lavender. She may come in dreadfully tired and hungry."

" But that would not vex her so much as the notion that you had waited on her account," said Sheila's husband, with a smile; and Mrs. Lorraine was pleased to hear him sometimes speak in a kindly way of the Highland girl whom he had married.

Lavender's guests were going somewhere after luncheon, and he had half promised to go with them, Mrs. Lorraine stipulating that Sheila should be induced to come also. But when luncheon was over, and Sheila had not appeared, he changed his intention. He would remain at home. He saw his three friends depart, and went into the study, and lit a cigar.

How odd the place seemed! Sheila had left no instructions about the removal of those barbaric decorations she had placed in the chamber; and here, around him, seemed to be the walls of the old-fashioned little room at Borvabost, with its big shells, its peacocks' feathers, its skins, and stuffed fish, and masses of crimson bell-heather. Was there not, too, an odour of peat-smoke in the air?—and then his eye caught sight of the plate that still stood on the window-sill, with the ashes of the burned peat on it.

"The odd child she is!" he thought, with a smile, "to go playing at grotto-making, and trying to fancy she was up in Lewis again. I suppose she would like to let her hair down again, and take off her shoes and stockings, and go wading along the sand in search of shellfish."

And then, somehow, his fancies went back to the old time when he had first seen and admired her wild ways, her fearless occupations by sea and shore, and the delight of active work that shone on her bright face and in her beautiful eyes. How lithe and handsome her figure used to be, in that blue dress, when she stood in the middle of the boat, her head bent back, her arms upstretched and pulling at some rope or other, and all the fine colour of exertion in the bloom of her cheeks! Then the pride with which she saw her little vessel cutting through the water—how she tightened her lips with a joyous determination as the sheets were hauled close and the gunwale of the small boat heeled over so that it almost touched the hissing and gurgling foam—how she laughed at Duncan's anxiety as she rounded some rocky point, and sent the boat spinning into the clear and smooth waters of the bay! Perhaps, after all, it was too bad to keep the poor child so long shut up in a city. She was evidently longing for a breath of sea-air, and for some brief dash of that brisk, fearless life on the sea-coast that she used to love. It was a happy life, after all; and he had himself enjoyed it, when his hands and face got browned by the sun, when he grew to wonder how any human being could wear black garments and drink foreign wines, and smoke cigars at eighteenpence apiece, so long as frieze coats, whisky, and a briar-root pipe were procurable. How one slept up in that remote island, after all the laughing, and drinking, and singing of the evening were over! How sharp was the monition of hunger when the keen sea-air blew about your face on issuing out in the morning; and how fresh, and cool, and sweet was that early breeze, with the scent of Sheila's flowers in it! Then the long, bright day at the river-side, with the black pools rippling in the wind, and in the silence the rapid whistle of the silken line through the air, and now and again the "blob" of a big salmon rising to a fly farther down the pool. Where was there any rest like the rest of the mid-day luncheon, when Duncan had put the big fish, wrapped in rushes, under the shadow of the nearest rock, when you sat down on the

warm heather, and lit your pipe, and began to
inquire where you had been bitten on hands and
neck by the ferocious " clegs " while you were
too busy in playing a fifteen pounder to care.
Then, perhaps, as you were sitting there in the
warm sunlight, with all the fresh scents of the
moorland around, you would hear a light foot-
step on the soft moss ; and, turning round, here
was Sheila herself, with a bright look in her
pretty eyes, and a half blush on her cheek, and a
friendly inquiry as to the way the fish had been
behaving. Then the beautiful, strange, cool
evenings on the shores of Loch Roag, with the
wild, clear light still shining in the northern
heavens, and the sound of the waves getting to
be lonely and distant ; or, still later, out in
Sheila's boat, with the great yellow moon rising
up over Suainabhal and Mealasabhal into a lambent vault of violet sky ; a pathway of quivering
gold lying across the loch ; a mild radiance
glittering here and there on the spars of the
small vessel, and, out there, the great Atlantic
lying still and distant as in a dream. As he sat
in this little room and thought of all these things,
he grew to think he had not acted quite fairly to
Sheila. She was so fond of that beautiful
island life ; and she had not even visited the
Lewis since her marriage. She should go now.

He would abandon that trip to the Tyrol; and as soon as arrangements could be made, they would together start for the north, and some day soon find themselves going up the steep shore to Sheila's home, with the old King of Borva standing in the porch of the house, and endeavouring to conceal his nervousness by swearing at Duncan's method of carrying the luggage.

Had not Sheila's stratagem succeeded? That pretty trick of hers, in decorating the room so as to resemble the house at Borvabost, had done all that she could have desired. But where was she?

Lavender rose hastily, and looked at his watch. Then he rang the bell, and a servant appeared.

"Did not Mrs. Lavender say when she would return?" he asked.

"No, sir."

"You don't know where she went?"

"No, sir. The young lady's luggage was put into the cab, and they drove away without leaving any message."

He scarcely dared confess to himself what fears began to assail him. He went upstairs to Sheila's room, and there everything appeared to be in its usual place, even to the smallest articles on the dressing-table. They were all there, except one. That was a locket, too large and clumsy to be worn, which someone had given her years before she left Lewis, and in which her father's portrait had been somewhat rudely set. Just after their marriage, Lavender had taken out this portrait, touched it up a bit into something of a better likeness, and put it back; and then she had persuaded him to have a photograph of himself coloured and placed on the opposite side. This locket, open and showing both portraits, she had fixed on to a small stand, and, in ordinary circumstances, it always stood on one side of her dressing-table. The stand was there; the locket was gone.

He went down stairs again. The afternoon was drawing on. A servant came to ask him at what hour he wished to dine; he bade her wait till her mistress came home, and consult her. Then he went out.

It was a beautiful, quiet afternoon, with a warm light from the west shining over the now yellowing trees of the squares and gardens. He walked down towards Notting Hill Gate Station, endeavouring to convince himself that he was not perturbed, and yet looking somewhat anxiously at the cabs that passed. People were now coming out from their business in the city, by train, and omnibus, and hansom; and they seemed to be hurrying home in very good spirits, as if they were sure of the welcome awaiting them there. Now and again you would see a meeting—some demure young person, who had been furtively watching the railway-station, suddenly showing a brightness in her face, as she went forward to shake hands with some new arrival, and then tripping briskly away with him, her hand on his arm. There were men carrying home fish in small bags, or baskets of fruit— presents to their wives, doubtless, from town. Occasionally an open carriage would go by, containing one grave and elderly gentleman and a group of small girls—probably his daughters, who had gone into the city to accompany their papa homeward. Why did these scenes and incidents, cheerful in themselves, seem to him to be somehow saddening, as he walked vaguely on? He knew, at least, that there was little use in returning home. There was no one in that silent house in the square. The rooms would be dark in the twilight. Probably dinner would be laid, with no one to sit down at the table. He wished Sheila had left word were she was going.

Then he bethought him of the way in which they had parted; and of the sense of fear that had struck him, the moment he left the

house, and after all he had been too harsh with
the child.   Now, at least, he was ready to
apologize to her.   If only he could see Sheila
coming along in one of those hansoms—if he
could see, at any distance, the figure he knew
so well walking towards him on the pavement—
would he not instantly confess to her that he
had been wrong, even grievously wrong, and
beg her to forgive him?   She should have it all
her own way about going up to Lewis.   He
would cast aside this Society-life he had been
living, and, to please her, would go in for any
sort of work or amusement of which she
approved.   He was so anxious, indeed, to put
these virtuous resolutions into force, that he
suddenly turned and walked rapidly back to the
house, with the wild hope that Sheila might
have already come back.

The windows were dark—the curtains were
yet drawn; and by this time the evening had
come on, and the lamps in the square had been
lit.   He let himself into the house by his latch-
key.   He walked into all the rooms, and up
into Sheila's room; everything remained as he
had left it.   The white cloth glimmered in the
dusk of the dining-room, and the light of the
lamp outside in the street touched here and
there the angles of the crystal and showed the

pale colours of the glasses. The clock on the mantelpiece ticked in the silence. If Sheila had been lying dead in that small room up-stairs, the house . could not have appeared more silent and solemn.

He could not bear this horrible solitude. He called one of the servants, and left a message for Sheila, if she came in in the interval, that he would be back at ten o'clock; then he went out, got into a hansom, and drove down to his club in St. James's Street.

Most of the men were dining; the other rooms were almost deserted. He did not care to dine just then. He went into the library; it was occupied by an old gentleman who was fast asleep in an easy-chair. He went into the billiard-rooms, in the vague hope that some exciting game might be going on; there was not a soul in the place, the gases were down, and an odour of stale smoke pervaded the dismal chambers. Should he go to the theatre? His sitting there would be a mockery, while this vague and terrible fear was present to his heart. Or go down to see Ingram, as had been his wont in previous hours of trouble? He dared not go near Ingram without some more definite news about Sheila. In the end, he went out into the open air, as if he were in danger of being stifled ; and, walking indeterminately on, found himself once more at his own house.

The place was still quite dark ; he knew before entering that Sheila had not returned, and he did not seem to be surprised. It was now long after their ordinary dinner-hour. When he went into the house he bade the servants light the gas and bring up dinner ; he would himself sit down at this solitary table, if only for the purpose of finding occupation and passing this terrible time of suspense.

It never occurred to him, as it might have occurred to him at one time, that Sheila had made some blunder somewhere and been una- voidably detained. He did not think of any possible repetition of her adventures in Rich- mond Park. He was too conscious of the pro- bable reason of Sheila's remaining away from her own home ; and yet, from minute to minute, he fought with that consciousness, and sought to prove to himself that, after all, she would soon be heard driving up to the door. He ate his dinner in silence ; and then drew a chair up to the fire and lit a cigar.

For the first time in his life he was driven to go over the events that had occurred since his marriage, and to ask himself how it had all come about that Sheila and he were not as they

once had been. He recalled the early days of
their friendship at Borva; the beautiful period
of their courtship; the appearance of the young
wife in London; and the close relegation of
Sheila to the domestic affairs of the house,
while he had chosen for himself other companions, other interests, other aims. There was
no attempt at self-justification in those com-
munings, but an effort, sincere enough in its
way, to understand how all this had happened.
He sat and dreamed there, before the warmth of
the fire, with the slow and monotonous ticking
of the clock unconsciously acting on his brain.
In time the silence, the warmth, the monotonous
sound, produced their natural effects, and he fell
fast asleep.

He awoke with a start. The small silver-
toned bell on the mantelpiece had struck the
hour of twelve. He looked around, and knew
that the evil had come upon him: for Sheila
had not returned, and all his most dreadful fears
of that evening were confirmed. Sheila had
gone away and left him—whither had she
gone?

Now there was no more indecision in his
actions. He got his hat, plunged into the cold
night air, and finding a hansom, bade the man
drive as hard as he could go down to Sloane

Street. There was a light in Ingram's windows, which were on the ground-floor ; he tapped with his stick on one of the panes—an old signal that had been in constant use when he and Ingram were close companions and friends. Ingram came to the door and opened it ; the light of a lamp glared in on his face.

"Hillo, Lavender!" he said, in a tone of surprise.

The other could not speak ; but he went into the house, and Ingram, shutting the door and following him, found that the man's face was deadly pale.

"Sheila——" he said, and stopped,

" Well, what about her ? " said Ingram, keeping quite calm, but with wild fancies about some terrible accident almost stopping the pulsation of his heart.

"Sheila has gone away."

Ingram did not seem to understand.

"Sheila has gone away, Ingram," said Lavender, in an excited way. "You don't know anything about it ? You don't know where she has gone ? What am I to do, Ingram—how am I to find her ? Good God, don't you understand what I tell you? And now it is past midnight, and my poor girl may be wandering about the streets."

He was walking up and down the room, paying almost no attention, in his excitement, to the small sallow-faced man, who stood quite quiet, a trifle afraid, perhaps, but with his heart full of a blaze of anger.

"She has gone away from your house," he said, slowly. "What made her do that?"

"I did," said Lavender, in a hurried way. "I have acted like a brute to her—that is true enough. You needn't say anything to me, Ingram; I feel myself far more guilty than anything you could say—you may heap reproaches on me afterwards—but tell me, Ingram, what am I to do. You know what a proud spirit she has—who can tell what she might do? She wouldn't go home—she would be too proud—she may have gone and drowned herself——"

"If you don't control yourself, and tell me what has happened, how am I to help you?" said Ingram, stiffly; and yet disposed somehow—perhaps for the sake of Sheila, perhaps because he saw that the young man's self-embarrassment and distress were genuine enough—not to be too rough with him.

"Well, you know Mairi," said Lavender, still walking up and down the room in an excited way: "Sheila had got up the girl here without telling me—some friends of mine were coming home to luncheon—we had some disagreement about Mairi being present—and then Sheila said something about not remaining in the house if Mairi did not—something of that sort. I don't know what it was, but I know it was all my fault; and if she has been driven from the house I did it—that is true enough. And where do you think she has gone, Ingram? If I could only see her for three minutes, I would explain everything; I would tell her how sorry I am for everything that has happened, and she would see, when she went back, how everything would be right again. I had no idea she would go away. It was mere peevishness that made me object to Mairi meeting those people; and I had no idea that Sheila would take it so much to heart. Now tell me what you think should be done, Ingram—all I want is to see her just for three minutes to tell her it was all a mistake, and that she will never have to fear anything like that again."

Ingram heard him out, and said, with some precision—

"Do you mean to say that you fancy all this trouble is to be got over that way? Do you know so little of Sheila, after the time you have been married to her, as to imagine that she has taken this step out of some momentary caprice, and that a few words of apology and promise will cause her to rescind it? You must be crazed, Lavender; or else you are actually as ignorant of the nature of that girl as you were up in the Highlands."

The young man seemed to calm down his excitement and impatience, but it was because of a new fear that had struck him, and that was visible in his face.

"Do you think she will never come back, Ingram?" he said, looking aghast.

"I don't know. She may not. At all events, you may be quite sure that, once having resolved to leave your house, she is not to be pacified and cajoled by a few phrases and a promise of repentance on your part. That is quite sure. And what is quite as sure is this, that if you knew just now where she was, the most foolish thing you could do would be to go and see her----"

"But I must go and see her—I must find her out, Ingram," he said, passionately. "I don't care what becomes of me. If she won't go back home, so much the worse for me; but I *must* find her out, and know that she is safe! Think of it, Ingram—perhaps she is walking about the streets somewhere at this moment—

and you know her proud spirit—if she were to go near the river——"

"She won't go near the river," said Ingram, quietly. "And she won't be walking about the streets. She is either in the Scotch mail-train, going up to Glasgow, or else she has got some lodgings somewhere, along with Mairi. Has she any money?"

"No," said Lavender. And then he thought for a minute. "There was some money her father gave her in case she might want it at a pinch—she may have that, I hope she has that. I was to have given her money to-morrow morning, But hadn't I better go to the police-stations, and see, just by way of precaution, that she has not been heard of? I may as well do that as nothing. I could not go home to that empty house. I could not sleep."

"Sheila is a sensible girl; she is safe enough," said Ingram. "And if you don't care about going home, you may as well remain here. I can give you a room up-stairs when you want it. In the meantime, if you will pull a chair to the table, and calm yourself, and take it for granted that you will soon be assured of Sheila's safety, I will tell you what I think you should do. Here is a cigar to keep you occupied; there is whisky and cold water back there, if you like; you will do no good by punishing yourself in small matters; for your trouble is likely to be serious enough, I can tell you, before you get Sheila back, if ever you get her back. Take the chair with the cushion."

It was so like the old days when these two used to be companions! Many and many a time had the younger man come down to these lodgings, with all his troubles, and wild impulses, and pangs of contrition ready to be revealed; and then Ingram, concealing the liking he had for the lad's generous waywardness, his brilliant and facile cleverness, and his dashes of honest self-depreciation, would gravely lecture him, and put him right, and send him off comforted. Frank Lavender had changed much since then. The handsome boy had grown into a man of the world; there was less self-revelation in his manner, and he was less sensitive to the opinions and criticisms of his old friend; but Ingram, who was not prone to idealism of any sort, had never ceased to believe that this change was but superficial, and that, in different circumstances and with different aims, Lavender might still fulfil the best promise of his youth.

"You have been a good friend to me, Ingram," he said, with a hot blush, "and I have treated you as badly as I have treated——By Jove, what a chance I had at one time!"

He was looking back on all the fair pictures his imagination had drawn while yet Sheila and he were wandering about that island in the northern seas.

"You had," said Ingram, decisively. "At one time I thought you the most fortunate man in the world. There was nothing left for you to desire, as far as I could see. You were young, and strong, with plenty of good spirits and sufficient ability to earn yourself an honourable living, and you had won the love of the most beautiful and best-hearted woman I have known. You never seemed to me to know what that meant. Men marry women—there is no difficulty about that; and you can generally get an amiable sort of person to become your wife, and have a sort of affection for you, and so on. But how many have bestowed on them the pure and exalted passion of a young and innocent girl, who is ready to worship with all the fervour of a warmly imaginative and emotional nature the man she has chosen to love? And suppose he is young, too, and capable of understanding all the tender sentiments of a high-spirited, sensitive, and loyal woman, and suppose that he fancies himself as much in love with her as she

with him? These conditions are not often ful-
filled, I can tell you. It is a happy fluke when
they are. Many a day ago I told you that you
should consider yourself more fortunate than if
you had been made an Emperor; and, indeed, it
seemed to me that you had everything in the
shape of worldly happiness easily within your
reach. How you came to kick away the ball from
your feet—well—God only knows. The thing
is inconceivable to me. You are sitting here as
you used to sit two or three years ago; and in
the interval you have had every chance in life;
and now if you are not the most wretched man
in London, you ought at least to be the most
ashamed and repentant."

Lavender's head was buried in his hands; he
did not speak.

"And it is not only your own happiness you
have destroyed. When you saw that girl first,
she was as light-hearted and contented with her
lot as any human being could be. From one
week's end to the other not the slightest care
disturbed her mind. And then, when she entrusted her whole life to you—when she staked
her faith in human nature on you, and gave you
all the treasures of hope and reverence, and love
that lay in her pure and innocent soul—my
God! what have you done with these? It is

not that you have shamed and insulted her as a wife, and driven her out of her home—there are other homes than yours where she would be welcome a thousand times over—but you have destroyed her belief in everything she had taught herself to trust, you have outraged the tenderest sentiments of her heart, you have killed her faith as well as ruined her life. I talk plainly. I cannot do otherwise. If I help you now, don't imagine I condone what you have done—I would cut off my right hand first. For Sheila's sake, I will try to help you."

He stopped just then, however, and checked the indignation that had got the better of his ordinarily restrained manner and curt speech. The man before him was crying bitterly, his face hidden in his hands.

"Look here, Lavender," he said, presently. "I don't want to be hard on you. I tell you plainly what I think of your conduct, so that no delusions may exist between us. And I will say this for you, that the only excuse you have——"

"There is no excuse," said the other, sadly enough. "I have no excuse, and I know it."

"The only thing, then, you can say in mitigation of what you have done is that you never seem to have understood the girl whom you

married. You started with giving her a fancy
character when first you went to the Lewis;
and once you had got the bit in your teeth,
there was no stopping you. If you seek now to
get Sheila back to you, the best thing you can
do, I presume, would be to try to see her as
she is, to win her regard that way, to abandon
that operatic business, and learn to know her as
a thoroughly good woman, who has her own
ways and notions about things, and who has a
very definite character underlying that extreme
gentleness which she fancies to be one of her
duties. The child did her dead best to accommo-
date herself to your idea of her, and failed. When
she would rather have been living a brisk and
active life in the country, or by the sea-side—
running wild about a hill-side, or reading strange
stories in the evening, or nursing some fisherman's child that had got ill—you had her dragged
into a sort of society with which she had no
sympathy whatever. And the odd thing to me
is that you yourself seemed to be making an
effort that way! You did not always devote
yourself to fashionable life. What became of all
your old ambitions you used to talk about in the
very chair you are now sitting in?"

"Is there any hope of my getting Sheila
back?" he said, looking up at last. There was

a vague and bewildered look in his eyes. He seemed incapable of thinking of anything but that.

"I don't know," said Ingram. "But one thing is certain—you will never get her back to repeat the experiment that has just ended in this desperate way."

"I should not ask that," he said, hurriedly. "I should not ask that at all. If I could but see her for a moment, I would ask her to tell me everything she wanted—everything she demanded as conditions—and I would obey them all. I will promise to do everything that she wishes."

"If you saw her, you could give her nothing but promises," said Ingram, quietly. "Now, what if you were to try to do what you know she wishes, and then go to her?"

"You mean——," said Lavender, glancing up with another startled look on his face. "You don't mean that I am to remain away from her a long time—go into banishment, as it were —and then, some day, come back to Sheila, and beg her to forget all that happened long before."

"I mean something very like that," said Ingram, with composure. "I don't know that it would be successful. I have no means of ascertaining what Sheila would think of such a project—whether she would think that she could ever live with you again."

Lavender seemed fairly stunned by the possibility of Sheila's resolving never to see him again; and began to recall what Ingram had many a time said about the strength of purpose she could show when occasion needed.

" If her faith in you is wholly destroyed, your case is hopeless. A woman may cling to her belief in a man, through good report and evil report; but if she once loses it, she never recovers it. But there is this hope for you. I know very well that Sheila had a much more accurate notion of you than ever you had of her; and I happen to know, also, that at the very time when you were most deeply distressing her, here in London, she held the firm conviction that your conduct towards her—your habits, your very self—would alter if you could only be persuaded to get out of the life you have been leading. That was true, at least, up to the time of your leaving Brighton. She believed in you then. She believed that if you were to cut Society altogether, and go and live a useful and hard-working life somewhere, you would soon become once more the man she fell in love with up in Lewis. Perhaps she was mistaken—I don't say anything about it myself."

The terribly cool way in which Ingram talked—separating, defining, exhibiting, so that he and his companion should get as near as possible to what he believed to be the truth of the situation—was oddly in contrast with the blind and passionate yearning of the other for some glimpse of hope. His whole nature seemed to go out in a cry to Sheila, that she would come back and give him a chance of atoning for the past. At length he rose. He looked strangely haggard, and his eyes scarcely seemed to see the things around him.

"I must go home," he said.

Ingram saw that he merely wanted to get outside and walk about in order to find some relief from this anxiety and unrest, and said—

"You ought, I think, to stop here and go to bed. But if you would rather go home, I will walk up with you, if you like."

When the two men went out, the night-air smelt sweet and moist, for rain had fallen, and the city trees were still dripping with the wet and rustling in the wind. The weather had changed suddenly, and now, in the deep blue overhead, they knew the clouds were passing swiftly by. Was it the coming light of the morning that seemed to give depth and richness to that dark blue vault, while the pavements of

the streets and the houses grew vaguely distinct
and grey?　Suddenly in turning the corner into
Piccadilly, they saw the moon appear in a rift of
those passing clouds; but it was not the moonlight that shed this pale and wan greyness down
the lonely streets.　It is just at this moment,
when the dawn of the new day begins to tell,
that a great city seems at its deadest; and in
the profound silence and amid the strange trans-
formations of the cold and growing light, a man
is thrown in upon himself, and holds communion
with himself, as though he and his own thoughts
were all that was left in the world.　Not a word
passed between the two men; and Lavender,
keenly sensitive to all such impressions, and now
and again shivering slightly, either from cold or
nervous excitement, walked blindly along the
deserted streets, seeing far other things than the
tall houses, and the drooping trees, and the
growing light of the sky.

It seemed to him at this moment that he was
looking at Sheila's funeral.　There was a great
stillness in that small house at Borvabost.
There was a boat—Sheila's own boat—down at
the shore there; and there were two or three
figures in black in it.　The day was grey and
rainy; the sea washed along the melancholy
shores; the far hills were hidden in mist.　And

now he saw some people come out of the house
into the rain, and the bronzed and bearded men
had oars with them, and on the crossed oars
there was a coffin placed. They went down the
hill-side. They put the coffin in the stern of
the boat; and in absolute silence—except for
the wailing of the women—they pulled away
down the dreary Loch Roag till they came to
the Island where the burial-ground is. They
carried the coffin up to that small enclosure,
with its rank grass growing green, and the rain
falling on the rude stones and memorials. How
often had he leaned on that low stone wall, and
read the strange inscriptions, in various tongues,
over the graves of mariners from distant countries who had met with their death on this rocky
coast. Had not Sheila herself pointed out to
him, with a sad air, how many of these memorials bore the words "who was drowned;" and
that, too, was the burden of the rudely-spelt
legends beginning with "Hier rutt in Gott,"
or "Her under hviler stovit," and sometimes
ending with the pathetic "Wunderschen ist unsre
Hoffnung." The fishermen brought the coffin to
the newly-made grave; the women standing
back a bit, old Scarlett MacDonald stroking
Mairi's hair, and bidding the girl control
her frantic grief, though the old woman herself

could hardly speak for her tears and her lamentations. He could read the words "Sheila Mackenzie" on the small silver plate: she had been taken away from all association with him and his name. And who was this old man with the white hair and the white beard, whose hands were tightly clenched, and his lips firm, and a look as of death in the sunken and wild eyes? Mackenzie was grey a year before——

"Ingram," he said, suddenly, and his voice startled his companion, "do you think it is possible to make Sheila happy again?"

"How can I tell?" said Ingram.

"You used to know everything she could wish—everything she was thinking about. If you find her out now, will you get to know? Will you see what I can do—not by asking her to come back, not by trying to get back my own happiness—but anything, it does not matter what it is, I can do for her? If she would rather not see me again, I will stay away. Will you ask her, Ingram?"

"We have got to find her first," said his companion.

"A young girl like that," said Lavender, taking no heed of the objection, "surely she cannot always be unhappy. She is so young and beautiful, and takes so much interest in many things—surely she may have a happy life."

"She might have had."

"I don't mean with me," said Lavender, with his haggard face looking still more haggard in the increasing light. "I mean anything that can be done—any way of life that will make her comfortable and contented again—anything that I can do for that, will you try to find it out, Ingram?"

"Oh yes, I will," said the other, who had been thinking with much foreboding of all these possibilities ever since they left Sloane Street, his only gleam of hope being a consciousness that this time at least there could be no doubt of Frank Lavender's absolute sincerity, of his remorse, and his almost morbid craving to make reparation if that were still possible.

They reached the house at last. There was a dim orange-coloured light shining in the passage. Lavender went on. and threw open the small room which Sheila had adorned, asking Ingram to follow him. How wild and strange this chamber looked, with the wan glare of the dawn shining in on its barbaric decorations from the sea-coast—on the shells, and skins, and feathers that Sheila had placed around! That wihte light of the morning was now shining

everywhere into the silent and desolate house.
Lavender found Ingram a bed-room; and then
he turned away, not knowing what to do. He
looked into Sheila's room: there were dresses,
bits of finery, and what not, that he knew so
well; but there was no light breathing audible
in the silent and empty chamber. He shut the
door, as reverently as though he were shutting it
on the dead; and went down-stairs and threw
himself almost fainting with despair and fatigue
on a sofa, while the world outside awoke to a
new day, with all its countless and joyous activi-
ties and duties.

CHAPTER II.

A SURPRISE.

THERE was no letter from Sheila in the morning; and Lavender, so soon as the post had come and gone, went up to Ingram's room and woke him.

"I am sorry to disturb you, Ingram," he said, "but I am going to Lewis. I shall catch the train to Glasgow at ten."

"And what do you want to get to Lewis for?" said Ingram, starting up. "Do you think Sheila would go straight back to her own people with all this humiliation upon her? And supposing she is not there, how do you propose to meet old Mackenzie?"

"I am not afraid of meeting any man," said Lavender; "I want to know where Sheila is. And if I see Mackenzie, I can only tell him frankly everything that has happened. He is not likely to say anything of me half as bad as what I think of myself."

"Now listen," said Ingram, sitting up in bed, with his brown beard and greyish hair in a considerably dishevelled condition. "Sheila may have gone home, but it isn't likely. If she has not, your taking the story up there, and spreading it abroad, would prepare a great deal of pain for her when she might go back at some future time. But suppose you want to make sure that she has not gone to her father's house. She could not have got down to Glasgow sooner than this morning, by last night's train, you know. It is to-morrow morning, not this morning, that the Stornoway steamer starts; and she would be certain to go direct to it at the Glasgow Broomielaw, and go round the Mull of Cantyre instead of catching it up at Oban, because she knows the people in the boat, and she and Mairi would be among friends. If you really want to know whether she has gone north, perhaps you could do no better than run down to Glasgow to-day, and have a look at the boat that starts to-morrow morning. I would go with you myself, but I can't escape the office to-day."

Lavender agreed to do this; and was about to go. But before he bade his friend good-bye, he lingered for a second or two in a hesitating way, and then he said—

"Ingram, you were speaking the other night of your going up to Borva. If you should go——."

"Of course I shan't go," said the other, promptly. "How could I face Mackenzie when he began to ask me about Sheila? No, I cannot go to Borva while this affair remains in its present condition; and, indeed, Lavender, I mean to stop in London till I see you out of your trouble somehow."

"You are heaping coals of fire on my head."

"Oh, don't look at it that way. If I can be of any help to you, I shall expect, this time, to have a return for it."

"What do you mean?"

"I will tell you when we get to know something of Sheila's intentions."

And so Frank Lavender found himself once more, as in the old times, in the Euston Station, with the Scotch mail ready to start, and all manner of folks bustling about with that unnecessary activity which betokens the excitement of a holiday. What a strange holiday was his! He got into a smoking-carriage in order to be alone; and he looked out on the people who were bidding their friends good-bye. Some of them were not very pretty; many of them were ordinary, insignificant, commonplace-looking folks;

but it was clear that they had those about
them who loved them and thought much of them.
There was one man whom, in other circumstances,
Lavender would have dismissed with contempt as
an excellent specimen of the unmitigated cad.
He wore a white waistcoat, purple gloves, and a
green sailor's knot with a diamond in it; and
there was a cheery, vacuous, smiling expression
on his round face as he industriously smoked a
cheroot and made small jokes to the friends who
had come to see him off. One of them was a
young woman, not very good-looking, perhaps,
who did not join in the general hilarity : and it
occurred to Lavender that the jovial man with
the cheroot was perhaps cracking his little jokes
to keep up her spirits. At all events he called
her " my good lass " from time to time, and
patted her on the shoulder, and was very kind to
her. And when the guard came up, and bade
everybody get in, the man kissed the girl, and
shook hands with her, and bade her good-bye;
and then she, moved by some sudden impulse,
caught his face in both her hands and kissed him
once on each cheek. It was a ridiculous scene.
People who wear green ties with diamond pins
care nothing for decorum. And yet Lavender,
when he averted his eyes from this parting, could
not help recalling what Ingram had been saying

the night before, and wondered whether this outrageous person, with his abominable decorations and his genial grin, might not be more fortunate than many a great statesman, or warrior, or monarch.

He turned round to find the cad beside him; and presently the man, with an abounding good nature, began to converse with him, and explained that it was 'igh 'oliday with him, for that he had got a pass to travel first-class as far as Carlisle. He hoped they would have a jolly time of it together. He explained the object of his journey in the frankest possible fashion; made a kindly little joke upon the hardship of parting with one's sweetheart; said that a faint heart never won fair lady, and that it was no good crying over spilt milk. She would be all right, and precious glad to see him back in three weeks' time, and he meant to bring her a present that would be good for sore eyes.

"Perhaps you're a married man, sir, and got past all them games?" said the cad, cheerily.

"Yes, I am married," said Lavender, coldly.

"And you're going further than Carlisle, you say, sir? I'll be sworn the good lady is up somewhere in that direction, and she won't be disappointed when she sees you—oh no! Scotch, sir?"

"I am not Scotch," said Lavender, curtly.

" And she ? "

Should he have to throw the man out of the window ?

" Yes."

" The Scotch are a strange race—very," said the genial person, producing a brandy flask. " They drink a trifle, don't they ; and yet they keep their wits about them if you've dealings with them. A very strange race of people in my opinion—very. Know the story of the master who fancied his man was drunk ? 'Donald, you're trunk,' says he. 'It's a tam lee,' says Donald. 'Donald, ye ken ye're trunk !' says the master. 'Ah ken ah wish to Kott ah wass !' says Donald. Good story, ain't it, sir ? "

Lavender had heard the remarkable old joke a hundred times ; but just at this moment there was something odd in this vulgar person suddenly imitating, and imitating very well, the Highland accent. Had he been away up in the north : or had he merely heard the story related by one who had been ? Lavender dared not ask, however, for fear of prolonging a conversation in which he had no wish to join. Indeed, to get rid of the man, he shoved a whole bundle of the morning papers into his hands.

" What's your opinion of politics at present, sir ? " observed his friend, in an off-hand way.

" I haven't any," said Lavender, compelled to take back one of the newspapers, and open it.

"I think, myself, they're in a bad state. That's my opinion. There ain't a man among 'em who knows how to keep down those people. That's my opinion, sir. What do you think?"

"Oh, I think so, too," said Lavender. "You'll find a good article in that paper on University Tests."

The cheery person looked rather blank.

"I would like to hear your opinion about 'em, sir," he said. "It ain't much good reading only one side of the question ; but when you can talk about it and discuss it, now——"

"I am sorry I can't oblige you," said Lavender, goaded into making some desperate effort to release himself. "I am suffering from relaxed throat at present. My doctor has warned me against talking too much."

"I beg your pardon, sir. You don't seem very well—perhaps the throat comes with a little feverishness, you see—a cold, in fact. Now, if I was you, I'd try tannin lozenges for the throat. They're uncommon good for the throat ; and a little quinine for the general system—that would put you as right as a fiver. I tried it myself when I was down in 'Ampshire last year. And you would'nt find a drop of this brandy a bad thing either, if you don't mind rowing in the same boat as myself."

Lavender declined the proffered flask, and subsided behind a newspaper. His fellow-traveller lit another cheroot, took up Bradshaw, and settled himself in a corner.

Had Sheila come up this very line some dozen hours before? Lavender asked himself, as he looked out on the hills, and valleys, and woods of Buckinghamshire. Had the throbbing of the engine and the rattle of the wheels kept the piteous eyes awake all through the dark night, until the pale dawn showed the girl a wild vision of northern hills and moors, telling her she was getting near to her own country? Not thus had Sheila proposed to herself to return home on the first holiday-time that should occur to them both. He began to think of his present journey as it might have been in other circumstances. Would she have remembered any of those pretty villages which she saw one early morning, long ago, when they were bathed in sunshine, and scarcely awake to the new day? Would she be impatient at the delays at the stations, and anxious to hurry on to Westmoreland and Dumfries, to Glasgow, and Oban, and Skye, and then from Stornoway across the island to the little inn at Garra-na-hina? Here, as he looked out of the window, the first indication of the wilder country became visible in the distant Berkshire hills. Close at hand the country lay green and bright under a brilliant sun; but over there in the east, some heavy clouds darkened the landscape, and the far hills seemed to be placed amid a gloomy stretch of moorland. Would not Sheila have been thrilled by this glimpse of the coming north? She would have fancied that greater mountains lay far behind these rounded slopes, hidden in mist. She would have imagined that no human habitations were near those rising plains of sombre hue, where the red-deer and the fox ought to dwell. And in her delight at getting away from the fancied brightness of the south, would she not have been exceptionally grateful and affectionate towards himself, and striven to please him with her tender ways?

It was not a cheerful journey—this lonely trip to the North. Lavender got to Glasgow that night; and next morning he went down, long before any passengers could have thought of arriving, to the *Clansman.* He did not go near the big steamer, for he was known to the captain and the steward; but he hung about the quays, watching each person who went on board. Sheila certainly was not among the passengers by the *Clansman.*

But she might have gone to Greenock, and waited for the steamer there. Accordingly, after the *Clansman* had started on her voyage, he went into a neighbouring hotel and had some breakfast, after which he crossed the bridge to the station, and took rail for Greenock, where he arrived some time before the *Clansman* made her appearance. He went down to the quay. It was yet early morning, and a cool fresh breeze was blowing in across the broad waters of the Firth, where the sunlight was shining on the white sails of the yachts and on the dipping and screaming sea-gulls. Far away beyond the pale blue mountains opposite lay the wonderful net-work of sea-loch and island through which one had to pass to get to the distant Lewis. How gladly, at this moment, would he have stepped on board the steamer, with Sheila, and put out on that gleaming plain of sea, knowing that by and by they would sail into Stornoway harbour and find the waggonette there. They would not hasten the voyage. She had never been round the Mull of Cantyre; and so he would sit by her side, and show her the wild tides meeting there, and the long jets of white foam shooting up the great wall of rocks. He would show her the pale coast of Ireland; and then they would see Islay, of which she had many a ballad and story. They would go through the narrow Sound that is overlooked by the gloomy mountains of Jura. They would see the distant islands where the chief of Colonsay is still mourned for on the still evenings, by the hapless mermaiden who sings her wild song across the sea. They would keep wide of the dangerous currents of Corryvreckan; and by and by they would sail into the harbour of Oban, the beautiful sea-town where Sheila first got a notion of the greatness of the world lying outside of her native island.

What if she were to come down now from this busy little seaport, which lay under a pale blue smoke, and come out upon this pier to meet the free sunlight and the fresh sea-air blowing all about? Surely at a great distance he could recognize the proud, light step, and the proud, sad face. Would she speak to him; or go past him, with firm lips and piteous eyes, to wait for the great steamer that was now coming along out of the eastern mist? Lavender glanced vaguely round the quays and the thoroughfares leading to them; but there was no one like Sheila there. In the distance he could hear the throbbing of the *Clansman's* engines, as the big steamer came on through the white plain. The sun was warmer now on the bright waters of the

Firth; and the distant haze over the pale blue mountains beyond had grown more luminous. Small boats went by; with here and there a yachtsman, scarlet-capped, and in white costume, taking a leisurely breakfast on deck. The seagulls circled about, or dipped down on the waters, or chased each other with screams and cries. Then the *Clansman* sailed into the quay, and there was a flinging of ropes, and general hurry and bustle, while people came crowding round the gangways, calling out to each other in every variety of dialect and accent.

Sheila was not there. He lingered about, and patiently waited for the starting of the steamer, not knowing how long she ordinarily remained at Greenock. He was in no hurry, indeed; for after the vessel had gone, he found himself with a whole day before him, and with no fixed notion as to how it could be passed.

In other circumstances, he would have been in no difficulty as to the spending of a bright forenoon and afternoon by the side of the sea. Or he could have run through to Edinburgh, and called on some artist-friends there. Or he could have crossed the Firth, and had a day's ramble among the mountains. But now that he was satisfied Sheila had not gone home, all his fancies and hopes went back to London. She

,as in London. And while he was glad she had not gone straight to her own people with a revelation of her wrongs, he scarcely dared speculate on what adventures and experiences might have befallen those two girls turned out into a great city, of which they were about equally ignorant.

The day passed somehow, and at night he was on his way to London. Next morning he went down to Whitehall, and saw Ingram.

"Sheila has not gone back to the Highlands, so far as I can make out," he said.

"So much the better," was the answer.

"What am I to do? She must be in London; and who knows what may befall her?"

"I cannot tell you what you should do. Of course you would like to know where she is; and I fancy she would have no objection herself to letting you know that she was all right, so long as she knew that you would not go near her. I don't think she has taken so decided a step merely for the purpose of being coaxed back again—that is not Sheila's way."

"I won't go near her," he said. "I only want to know that she is safe and well. I will do whatever she likes; but I must know where she is, and that she has come to no harm."

"Well," said Ingram, slowly, "I was talking

the matter over with Mrs. Lorraine last
night——"

"Does *she* know?" said Lavender, wincing
somewhat.

"Certainly," Ingram answered. "I did not
tell her. I had promised to go up there about
something quite different, when she immediately
began to tell me the news. Of course it was
impossible to conceal such a thing. Don't all
the servants about know?"

"I don't care who knows," said Lavender,
moodily. "What does Mrs. Lorraine say about
this affair?"

"Mrs. Lorraine says that it serves you right,"
said Ingram, bluntly.

"Thank her very much. I like candour,
especially in a fair-weather friend."

"Mrs. Lorraine is a better friend to you than
you imagine," Ingram said, taking no notice of
the sneer. "When she thought that your going
to their house continually was annoying Sheila,
she tried to put a stop to it for Sheila's sake.
And now, at this very moment, she is doing her
very best to find out where Sheila is; and if she
succeeds, she means to go and plead your cause
with the girl."

"I will not have her do anything of the
kind," said Lavender, fiercely. "I will plead

my own cause with Sheila. I will have forgiveness from Sheila herself alone—not brought to me by any intermeddling woman."

"You needn't call names," said Ingram, coolly. "But I confess I think you are right; and I told Mrs. Lorraine that was what you would doubtless say. In any case, she can do no harm in trying to find out where Sheila is."

"And how does she propose to succeed? Pollaky? The 'Agony' Column? Placards, or a Bellman? I tell you, Ingram, I won't have that woman meddle in my affairs—coming forward as a sister of mercy to heal the wounded—bestowing mock compassion, and laughing all the time——"

"Lavender, you are beside yourself. That woman is one of the most good-natured, shrewd, clever, and amiable women I have ever met. What has enraged you?"

"Bah! She has got hold of you too, has she? I tell you she is a rank impostor."

"An impostor!" said Ingram slowly. "I have heard a good many people called impostors. Did it ever occur to you that the blame of the imposture might possibly lie with the person imposed on? I have heard of people falling into the delusion that a certain modest and simple-minded man was a great politician or a great

wit, although he had never claimed to be anything of the kind ; and then, when they found
out that in truth he was just what he had pretended to be, they called out against him as an
impostor. I have heard, too, of young gentlemen accusing women of imposture whose only
crime was, that they did not possess qualities
which they had never pretended to possess, but
which the young gentlemen fancied they ought
to possess. Mrs. Lorraine may be an impostor
to you. I think she is a thoroughly good
woman, and I know she is a very delightful
companion. And if you want to know how she
means to find Sheila out, I can tell you. She
thinks that Sheila would probably go to an
hotel, but that afterwards she would try to find
lodgings with some of the people whom she had
got to know through her giving them assistance.
Mrs. Lorraine would like to ask your servants
about the women who used to come for this
help. Then, she thinks, Sheila would probably
get some one of these humble friends to call for
her letters, for she would like to hear from her
father, and she would not care to tell him that
she had left your house. There is a great deal
of supposition in all this ; but Mrs. Lorraine is
a shrewd woman, and I would trust her instinct
in such matters a long way. She is quite sure

that Sheila would be too proud to tell her father, and very much averse, also, to inflicting so severe a blow on him——"

" But surely," Lavender said, hastily, " if Sheila wishes to conceal this affair for a time, she must believe it to be only temporary? She cannot propose to make the separation final ? "

" That I don't know anything about. I would advise you to go and see Mrs. Lorraine."

" I won't go and see Mrs. Lorraine."

" Now, this is unreasonable, Lavender. You begin to fancy that Sheila had some sort of dislike to Mrs. Lorraine, founded on ignorance; and straightway you think it is your duty to go and hate the woman. Whatever you may think of her, she is willing to do you a service."

" Will you go, Ingram, and take her to those servants ? "

" Certainly, I will, if you commission me to do so," said Ingram, readily.

" I suppose they all know ? "

" They do."

" And everyone else ? "

" I should think few of your friends would remain in ignorance of it."

" Ah, well," said Lavender, " if only I could get Sheila to overlook what is past, this once, I should not trouble my dear friends and acquaintances for their sympathy and condolence. By the time I saw them again, I fancy they would have forgotten our names."

There was no doubt of the fact that the news of Sheila's flight from her husband's house had travelled very speedily round the circle of Lavender's friends, and doubtless, in due time, it reached the ears of his aunt. At all events, Mrs. Lavender sent a message to Ingram, asking him to come and see her. When he went, he found the little, dry, hard-eyed woman in a terrible passion. She had forgotten all about Marcus Aurelius, and the composure of a philosopher, and the effect of anger on the nervous system. She was bolstered up in bed, for she had had another bad fit; but she was brisk enough in her manner and fierce enough in her language.

"Mr. Ingram," she said, the moment he had entered, "do you consider my nephew a beast?"

"I don't," he said.

"I do," she retorted.

"Then you are quite mistaken, Mrs. Lavender. Probably you have heard some exaggerated story of all this business. He has been very inconsiderate and thoughtless, certainly; but I don't believe he quite knew how sensitive his wife was ; and he is very repentant now, and I know he will keep his promises."

"You would apologize for the devil," said the little old woman, frowning.

"I would try to give him his due, at all events," said Ingram, with a laugh. "I know Frank Lavender very well—I have known him for years ; and I know there is good stuff in him, which may be developed in proper circumstances. After all, what is there more common than for a married man to neglect his wife ? He only did unconsciously and thoughtlessly what heaps of men do deliberately."

"You are making me angry," said Mrs. Lavender, in a severe voice.

"I don't think it fair to expect men to be demigods," Ingram said, carelessly. "I never met any demigods myself ; they don't live in my neighbourhood. Perhaps if I had had some experience of a batch of them, I should be more censorious of other people. If you set up Frank for a Bayard, is it his fault, or yours ? "

"I am not going to be talked out of my common sense, and me on my death-bed," said the old lady, impatiently, and yet with some secret hope that Ingram would go on talking and amuse her. "I won't have you say he is anything but a stupid and ungrateful boy, who married a wife far too good for him. He is worse than that—he is much worse than that; but as this may be my death-bed, I will keep a civil tongue in my head."

" I thought you did not like his wife very much ? " said Ingram.

" I am not bound to like her because I think badly of him, am I ? She was not a bad sort of girl, after all—temper a little stiff, perhaps; but she was honest. It did one's eyes good to look at her bright face. Yes, she was a good sort of creature in her way. But when she ran off from him, why didn't she come to me ? "

" Perhaps you never encouraged her."

" Encouragement ! Where ought a married woman go to but to her husband's relatives ? If she cannot stay with him, let her take the next best substitute. It was her duty to come to me."

" If Sheila had fancied it to be her duty, she would have come here, at any cost."

" What do you mean, Mr. Ingram ? " said Mrs. Lavender, severely.

" Well, supposing she didn't like you——" he was beginning to say, cautiously, when she sharply interrupted him.

" She didn't like me, eh ? "

" I said nothing of the kind. I was about to

say that if she had thought it her duty to come here, she would have come, in any circumstances."

"She might have done worse. A young woman risks a great deal in running away from her husband's home. People will talk. Who is to make people believe just the version of the story that the husband or wife would prefer?"

"And what does Sheila care," said Ingram, with a hot flush in his face, "for the belief of a lot of idle gossips and slanderers?"

"My dear Mr. Ingram," said the old lady, "you are not a woman, and you don't know the bother one has to look after one's reputation. But that is a question not likely to interest you. Let us talk of something else. Do you know why I wanted you to come and see me to-day?"

"I am sure I don't."

"I mean to leave you all my money."

He stared. She did not appear to be joking. Was it possible that her rage against her nephew had carried her to this extreme resolve?

"Oh!" he stammered; "but I won't have it, Mrs. Lavender."

"But you'll have to have it," said the little old woman, severely. "You are a poor man. You could make good use of my money—better than a charity board—that would starve the poor with

a penny out of each shilling, and spend the other
elevenpence in treating their friends to flower-
shows and dinners. Do you think I mean to leave
my money to such people? You shall have it.
I think you would look very well driving a mail-
phaeton in the Park; and I suppose you would
give up your pipes and your philosophy, and
your bachelor walks into the country. You
would marry, of course—every man is bound to
make 'a fool of himself that way, as soon as he
gets enough money to do it with. But perhaps
you might come across a clever and sensible
woman, who would look after you, and give
you your own way while having her own. Only
don't marry a fool. Whatever you do, don't
marry a fool, or all your philosophers won't
make the house bearable to you."

"I am not likely to marry anybody, Mrs.
Lavender," said Ingram, carelessly.

"Is there no woman you know whom you
would care to marry?"

"Oh," he said, "there is one woman—yes—
who seems to me about everything that a man
could wish; but the notion of my marrying her
is absurd. If I had known in time, don't you
see, that I should ever think of such a thing, I
should have begun years ago to dye my hair. I
can't begin now. Grey hair inspires reverence,

I believe ; but it is a bad thing to go **courting** with."

" You must not talk foolishly," said the little old lady, with a frown. " Do you think a sensible woman wants to marry a boy, who will torment her with his folly, and his empty head, and his running after a dozen different women ? Grey hair ! If you think grey hair is a bad thing to go courting with, I will give you something better. I will put something in your hand that will make the young lady forget your grey hair. Oh, of course, you will say that she cannot be tempted; that she despises money. If so, so much the better ; but I have known more women than you, and my hair is greyer than yours ; and you will find that a little money won't stand in the way of your being accepted."

He had made some gesture of protest, not against her speaking of his possible marriage, which scarcely interested him, so remote was the possibility, but against her returning to this other proposal. And when he saw the old woman really meant to do this thing, he found it necessary to declare himself explicitly on the point.

" Oh, don't imagine, Mrs. Lavender," he said, " that I have any wild horror of money, or that I suppose anybody else would have. I should like to have five times, or ten times as much as you seem generously disposed to give me. But here is the point, you see. I am a vain person. I am very proud of my own opinion of myself; and, if I acceded to what you propose—if I took your money—I suppose I should be driving about in that fine phaeton you speak of. That is very good—I like driving, and I should be pleased with the appearance of the trap and the horses. But what do you fancy I should think of myself—what would be my opinion of my own nobleness, and generosity, and humanity—if I saw Sheila Mackenzie walking by on the pavement, without any carriage to drive in, perhaps without a notion as to where she was going to get her dinner? I should be a great hero to myself then, shouldn't I?"

"Oh, Sheila again!" said the old woman, in a tone of vexation. "I can't imagine what there is in that girl to make men rave so about her. That Jew-boy is become a thorough nuisance—you would fancy she had just stepped down out of the clouds to present him with a gold harp, and that he couldn't look up to her face. And you are just as bad. You are worse—for you don't blow it off in steam. Well, there need be no difficulty. I meant to leave the girl in your charge. You take the money and look after her—I know she won't starve. Take it in trust for her, if you like."

"But that is a fearful responsibility, Mrs. Lavender," he said, in dismay. "She is a married woman. Her husband is the proper person——"

"I tell you I won't give him a farthing!" she said, with a sudden sharpness that startled him. "Not a farthing! If he wants money, let him work for it, as other people do; and then, when he has done that, if he is to have any of my money, he must be beholden for it to his wife and to you."

"Do you think that Sheila would accept anything that she would not immediately hand over to him?"

"Then he must come first to you."

"I have no wish to inflict humiliation on anyone," said Ingram, stiffly. "I don't wish to play the part of a little Providence, and mete out punishment in that way. I might have to begin with myself."

"Now, don't be foolish," said the old lady, with a menacing composure. "I give you fair warning. The next fit will do for me. If you don't care to take my money, and keep it in trust for this girl you profess to care so much about, I will leave it to found an institution.

And I have a good idea for an institution, mind you. I mean to teach people what they should eat and drink, and the various effects of food on various constitutions."

"It is an important subject," Ingram admitted.

"Is it not? What is the use of giving people laborious information about the idle fancies of generations that lived ages before they were born, while you are letting them poison their system, and lay up for themselves a fearfully painful old age, by the continuous use of unsuitable food? That book you gave me, Mr. Ingram, is a wonderful book; but it gives you little consolation if you know another fit is coming on. And what is the good of knowing about Epictetus, and Zeno, and the rest, if you've got rheumatism? Now I mean to have classes, to teach people what they should eat and drink— and I'll do it, if you won't assume the guardianship of my nephew's wife."

"But this is the wildest notion I ever heard of!" Ingram protested again. "How can I take charge of her? If Sheila herself had shown any disposition to place herself under your care, it might have been different."

"Oh, it would have been different!" cried the old lady, with a shrill laugh. "It would

have been different! And what did you say
about her sense of duty to her husband's relatives? Did you say anything about that?"

"Well——" Ingram was about to say, being
lost in amazement at the odd glee of this
withered old creature.

"Where do you think a young wife should
go, if she runs off from her husband's house?"
cried Mrs. Lavender, apparently much amused
by his perplexity. "Where can she best escape
calumny? Poor man! I won't frighten you, or
disturb you any longer. Ring the bell, will
you? I want Paterson."

Ingram rang.

"Paterson," said Mrs. Lavender, when the
tall and grave woman appeared, "ask Mrs.
Lavender if she can come here for a few
minutes."

Ingram looked at the old woman, to see if she
had gone mad; and then, somehow, he instinctively turned to the door. He fancied he knew
that quick, light step. And then, before he
well knew how, Sheila had come forward to him,
with her hands outstretched, and with something
like a smile on her pale face. She looked at him
for a second; she tried to speak to him, but
there was a dangerous quivering of the lips;
and then she suddenly burst into tears, and let

go his hands and turned away. In that brief moment he had seen what havoc had been wrought within the past two or three days. There were the same proud and handsome features, but they were pale and wan; and there was a piteous and weary look in the eyes, that told of the trouble and heartrending of sleepless nights.

"Sheila," he said, following her and taking her hand, " does anyone know of your being here ? "

" No," she said, still holding her head aside, and downcast; " no one. And I do not wish anyone to know. I am going away."

" Where ? "

" Don't you ask too much, Mr. Ingram," said the old lady, from amid her cushions and curtains. " Give her that ammonia—the stopper only. Now, sit down, child; and dry your eyes. You need not be ashamed to show Mr. Ingram that you knew where you ought to come to when you left your husband's house. And if you won't stop here, of course I can't compel you; though Mr. Ingram will tell you you might do worse."

" Sheila, why do you wish to go away? Do you mean to go back to the Lewis ? "

" Oh ! no, no ! " she said, almost shuddering.

" Where do you wish to go ? "

" Anywhere — it does not matter. But I cannot remain here. I should meet with — with many people I used to know. Mrs. Lavender, she is kind enough to say she will get me some place, for Mairi and me — that is all as yet that is settled."

" Is Mairi with you ? "

" Yes ; I will go and bring her to you. It is not anyone in London she will want to see as much as you."

Sheila left the room, and by and by came back, leading the young Highland girl by the hand. Mairi was greatly embarrassed, scarcely knowing whether she should show any gladness at meeting this old friend amid so much trouble. But when Ingram shook hands with her, and after she had blushed, and looked shy, and said, " And are you ferry well, sir ? " she managed somehow to lift her eyes to his face ; and then she said, suddenly —

" And it is a good day, this day, for Miss Sheila, that you will come to see her, Mr. Ingram ; for she will hef a friend now."

" You silly girl," said Mrs. Lavender, sharply, " why will you say ' Miss Sheila ' ? Don't you know she is a married woman ? "

Mairi glanced in a nervous and timid manner

towards the bed. She was evidently afraid of the little shrivelled old woman with the staring black eyes and the harsh voice.

" Mairi hasn't forgotten her old habits, that is all," said Ingram, patting her good-naturedly on the head.

And then he sat down again ; and it seemed so strange to him to see these two together again, and to hear the odd infection of Mairi's voice, that he almost forgot that he had made a great discovery in learning of Sheila's where-abouts, and wholly forgot that he had just been offered, and had just refused, a fortune.

CHAPTER III.

MEETING AND PARTING.

THE appearance of Sheila in Mrs. Lavender's house certainly surprised Ingram; but the motives which led her to go thither were simple enough. On the morning on which she had left her husband's house, she and Mairi had been driven up to Euston Square Station before she seemed capable of coming to any decision. Mairi guessed at what had happened, with a great fear at her heart, and did not dare to speak of it. She sat, mute and frightened, in a corner of the cab, and only glanced from time to time at her companion's pale face and troubled and distant eyes.

They were driven in to the station. Sheila got out, still seeming to know nothing of what was around her. The cabman took down Mairi's trunk, and handed it to a porter.

"Where for, miss?" said the man. And she started.

"Where will you be going, Miss Sheila?" said Mairi, timidly.

"It is no matter just now," said Sheila to the porter, "if you will be so kind as to take charge of the trunk. And how much must I pay the cabman from Notting Hill?"

She gave him the money, and walked into the great stone-paved hall, with its lofty roof and sounding echoes.

"Mairi," she said, "I have gone away from my own home, and I have no home for you or myself either. What are we to do?"

"Are you quite sure, Miss Sheila," said the girl, dismayed beyond expression, "that you will not go back to your own house? It wass a bad day this day that I wass come to London to find you going away from your own house?"

And Mairi began to cry.

"Will we go back to the Lewis, Miss Sheila?" she said. "It is many a one there will be proud and pleased to see you again in sa Lewis, and there will be plenty of homes for you there—oh, yes! ferry many that will be glad to see you! And it was a bad day sa day you left the Lewis whatever; and if you will go back again, Miss Sheila, you will neffer hef to go away again not any more."

Sheila looked at the girl—at the pretty pale

face, the troubled light-blue eyes, and the abundant fair-yellow hair. It was Mairi, sure enough, who was talking to her; and yet it was in a strange place. There was no sea dashing outside—no tide running in from the Atlantic. And where was old Scarlett, with her complaints, and her petulance, and her motherly kindness?

"It is a pity you have come to London, Mairi," Sheila said, wistfully; "for I have no house to take you into; and we must go now and find one."

"You will not go back to sa Lewis, Miss Sheila?"

"They would not know me in the Lewis any more, Mairi. I have been too long away, and I am quite changed. It is many a time I will think of going back; but when I left the Lewis, I was married; and now—— How could I go back to the Lewis, Mairi? They would look at me. They would ask questions. My father would come down to the quay, and he would say, 'Sheila have you come back alone?' And all the story of it would go about the island, and everyone would say I had been a bad wife, and my husband had gone away from me."

"There is not anyone," said Mairi, with the tears starting to her eyes again, "not from end of sa island to sa other, would say that of you,

Miss Sheila ; and there is no one would not come to meet you, and be glad sat you will come again to your own home. And as for going back, I will be ferry glad to go back whatever, for it was you I wass come to see, and not any town ; and I do not like this town, what I hef seen of it, and I will be ferry glad to go away wis you, Miss Sheila."

Sheila did not answer. She felt that it was impossible she could go back to her own people with this disgrace upon her, and did not even argue the question with herself. All her trouble now was to find some harbour of refuge into which she could flee, so that she might have quiet, and solitude, and an opportunity of studying all that had befallen her. The noise around her—the arrival of travellers, the transference of luggage, the screaming of trains—stunned her and confused her ; and she could only vaguely think of all the people she knew in London, to see to whom she could go for advice and direction. They were not many. One after the other she went over the acquaintances she had made ; and not one of them appeared to her in the light of a friend. One friend she had, who would have rejoiced to have been of the least assistance to her ; but her husband had forbidden her to hold communication with him, and she felt a strange sort of pride, even at this moment, in resolving to obey that injunction. In all this great city that lay around her, there was no other to whom she could frankly and readily go. That one friend she had possessed before she came to London; in London, she had not made another.

And yet it was necessary to do something; for who could tell but that her husband might come to this station in search of her? Mairi's anxiety, too, was increasing every moment; insomuch that she was fairly trembling with excitement and fatigue. Sheila resolved that she would go down and throw herself on the tender mercies of that terrible old lady in Kensington Gore. For one thing, she instinctively sought the help of a woman in her present plight; and perhaps this harshly-spoken old lady would be gentle to her when all her story was told. Another thing that prompted this decision was a sort of secret wish to identify herself even yet with her husband's family; to prove to herself, as it were, that they had not cast her off as being unworthy of him. Nothing was further from her mind at this moment than any desire to pave the way for reconciliation and reunion with her husband. Her whole anxiety was to get away from him; to put an end to a state of things which she had found to be more than she could bear.

And yet, if she had had friends in London called respectively Mackenzie and Lavender, and if she had been equally intimate with both, she would at this moment have preferred to go for help to those bearing the name of Lavender.

There was doubtless something strangely inconsistent in this instinct of wifely loyalty and duty in a woman who had just voluntarily left her husband's house. Lavender had desired her not to hold communication with Edward Ingram; even now she would respect his wish. Lavender would prefer that she should, in any great extremity, go to his aunt for assistance and counsel; and to his aunt, despite her own dislike of the woman, she would go. At this moment, when Sheila's proud spirit had risen up in revolt against a system of treatment that had become insufferable to her, when she had been forced to leave her home and incur the contemptuous compassion of friends and acquaintances, if Edward Ingram himself had happened to meet her, and had begun to say hard things of Lavender, she would have sharply recalled him to a sense of the discretion that one must use in speaking to a wife of her husband.

The two homeless girls got into another cab, and were driven down to Kensington Gore. Sheila asked if she could see Mrs. Lavender.

She knew that the old lady had had another bad fit; but she was supposed to be recovering rapidly. Mrs. Lavender would see her in her bedroom; and so Sheila went up.

The girl could not speak.

" Yes, I see it—something wrong about that precious husband of yours," said the old lady, watching her keenly. " I expected it. Go on. What is the matter?"

" I have left him," Sheila said, with her face very pale, but no sign of emotion about the firm lips.

" Oh, good gracious, child! Left him? How many people know it?"

" No one, but yourself, and a young Highland girl who has come up to see me."

" You came to me first of all?"

" Yes."

" Have you no other friends to go to?"

" I considered that I ought to come to you."

There was no cunning in the speech; it was the simple truth. Mrs. Lavender looked at her hard for a second or two, and then said, in what she meant to be a kind way—

" Come here, and sit down, child; and tell me all about it. If no one else knows it, there is no harm done. We can easily patch it up before it gets abroad."

"I did not come to you for that, Mrs. Lavender," said Sheila, calmly. "That is impossible. That is all over. I have come to ask you where I may get lodgings for my friend and myself."

"Tell me all about it, first : and then we'll see whether it can't be mended. Mind, I am ready to be on your side, though I am your husband's aunt. I think you're a good girl—a bit of a temper, you know—but you manage to keep it quiet ordinarily. You tell me all about it; and you'll see if I haven't means to bring him to reason. Oh, yes—oh, yes—I'm an old woman ; but I can find some means to bring him to reason." And she laughed an odd, shrill laugh.

A hot flush came over Sheila's face. Had she come to this old woman only to make her husband's degredation more complete? Was he to be intimidated into making friends with her by a threat of the withdrawal of that money that Sheila had begun to detest ? And this was what her notions of wifely duty had led to !

"Mrs. Lavender," she said, with the proud lips very proud indeed, " I must say this to you before I tell you anything. It is very good of you to say you will take my side ; but I did not come to you to complain. And I would rather not have any sympathy from you if it only means that you will speak ill of my husband. And if you think you can make him do things because you give him money—perhaps that is true at present; but it may not always be true, and you cannot expect me to wish it to continue. I would rather have my present trouble twenty times over than see him being bought over to any woman's wishes."

Mrs. Lavender stared at her.

" Why, you astonishing girl, I believe you are still in love with that man."

Sheila said nothing.

" Is it true ? " she said.

" I suppose a woman ought to love her husband," Sheila answered.

" Even if he turns her out of the house ? "

" Perhaps it is she who is to blame," Sheila said, humbly. " Perhaps her education was wrong—or she expects too much that is unreasonable—or perhaps she has a bad temper. You think I have a bad temper, Mrs. Lavender ; and might it not be that ? "

" Well, I think you want your own way ; and doubtless you expect it now. I suppose I am to listen to all your story, and I must not say a word about my own nephew. But sit down and tell me all about it ; and then you can justify him afterwards, if you like."

It was probably, however, the notion that Sheila would try to justify Lavender all through that put the old lady on her guard, and made her, indeed, regard Lavender's conduct in an unfairly bad light. Sheila told the story as simply as she could, putting everything down to her husband's advantage that was possible, and asking for no sympathy whatsoever. She only wanted to remain away from his house; and by what means could she and this young cousin of hers find cheap lodgings where they could live quietly, and without much fear of detection?

Mrs. Lavender was in a rage; and, as she was not allowed to vent it on the proper object, she turned upon Sheila herself.

"The Highlanders are a proud race," she said, sharply. "I should have thought that rooms in this house, even with the society of a cantankerous old woman, would have been tolerated for a time."

"It is very kind of you to make the offer," Sheila said, "but I do not wish to have to meet my husband or any of his friends. There is enough trouble without that. If you could tell me where to get lodgings not far from this neighbourhood, I would come to see you sometimes at such hours as I know he cannot be here."

"But I don't understand what you mean. You won't go back to your husband—although I could manage that for you directly. You won't hear of negotiations, or of any prospect of your going back; and yet you won't go home to your father."

"I cannot do either," Sheila said.

"Do you mean to live in those lodgings always?"

"How can I tell?" said the girl, piteously. "I only wish to be away; and I cannot go back to my papa, with all this story to tell him."

"Well, I didn't want to distress you," said the old woman. "You know your own affairs best. I think you are mad. If you would calmly reason with yourself, and show to yourself that, in a hundred years, or less than that, it won't matter whether you gratified your pride or no, you would see that the wisest thing you can do now is to take an easy and comfortable course. You are in an excited and nervous state at present, for example; and that is destroying so much of the vital portion of your frame. If you go into these lodgings, and live like a rat in a hole, you will have nothing to do but nurse these sorrows of yours, and find them grow bigger and bigger, while you grow more and more wretched. All that is mere pride, and sentiment, and folly. On the other hand, look at this. Your husband is sorry you are away from him—you may take that for granted. You say he was merely thoughtless; now he has got something to make him think, and would without doubt come and beg your pardon, if you gave him a chance. I write to him; he comes down here; you kiss and make good friends again, and to-morrow morning you are comfortable and happy again."

"To-morrow morning?" said Sheila, sadly. "Do you know how we should be situated to-morrow morning? The story of my going away would become known to his friends; he would go among them as though he had suffered some disgrace, and I the cause of it. And though he is a man, and would soon be careless of that, how could I go with him amongst his friends, and feel that I had shamed him? It would be worse than ever between us; and I have no wish to begin again what ended this morning—none at all, Mrs. Lavender."

"And do you mean to say that you intend to live permanently apart from your husband?"

"I do not know," said Sheila, in a despairing tone. "I cannot tell you. What I feel is that, with all this trouble, it is better that our life as it was in that house should come to an end."

Then she rose.   There was a tired look about her face, as if she were too weary to care whether this old woman would help her or no.   Mrs. Lavender regarded her for a moment, wondering, perhaps, that a girl so handsome, fine-coloured, and proud-eyed, should be distressing herself with imaginary sentiments, instead of taking life cheerfully, enjoying the hour as it passed, and being quite assured of the interest, and liking, and homage of everyone with whom she came in contact.   Sheila turned to the bed once more, about to say that she had troubled Mrs. Lavender too much already, and that she would look after these lodgings.   But the old woman apparently anticipated as much, and said, with much deliberation, that if Sheila and her companion would only remain one or two days in the house, proper rooms should be provided for them somewhere.   Young girls could not venture into lodgings without strict inquiries being made. Sheila should have suitable rooms; and Mrs. Lavender would see that she was properly looked after, and that she wanted for nothing.   In the meantime she must have some money.

"It is kind of you," said the girl, blushing hotly, "but I do not require it."

"Oh, I suppose we are too proud!" said the old woman.   "If we disapprove of our husband taking money, we must not do it either. Why, child, you have learnt nothing in London. You are a savage yet. You must let me give you something for your pocket, or what are you to do? You say you have left everything at home; do you think hair-brushes, for example, grow on trees, that you can go into Kensington Gardens and stock your rooms?"

"I have some money—a few pounds—that my papa gave me," Sheila said.

"And when that is done?"

"He will give me more."

"And yet you don't wish him to know you have left your husband's house! What will he make of these repeated demands for money?"

"My papa will give me anything I want, without asking any questions."

"Then he is a bigger fool than I expected. Oh, don't get into a temper again. Those sudden shocks of colour, child, show me that your heart is out of order. How can you expect to have a regular pulsation if you flare up at anything anyone may say? Now go and fetch me your Highland cousin."

Mairi came into the room in a very timid fashion, and stared with her big, light-blue eyes into the dusky recess in which the little old woman sat up in bed. Sheila took her forward.

"This is my cousin Mairi, Mrs. Lavender."

"And are you ferry well, ma'am?" said Mairi, holding out her hand very much as a boy pretends to hold out his hand to a tiger in the Zoological Gardens.

"Well, young lady," said Mrs. Lavender, staring at her, "and a pretty mess *you* have got us into!"

"Me!" said Mairi, almost with a cry of pain: she had not imagined before that she had anything to do with Sheila's trouble.

"No, no, Mairi," her companion said, taking her hand; "it was not you. Mrs. Lavender, Mairi does not understand our way of joking in London. Perhaps she will learn before she goes back to the Highlands."

"There is one thing," said Mrs. Lavender, observing that Mairi's eyes had filled the moment she was charged with bringing trouble on Sheila. "there is one thing you people from the Highlands seem never disposed to learn, and that is, to have a little control over your passions. If one speaks to you a couple of words, you either begin to cry or go off into a flash of rage. Don't you know how bad that is for the health?"

"And yet," said Sheila, with a smile—and it seemed so strange to Mairi to see her smile—

" we will not compare badly in health with the people about us here."

Mrs. Lavender dropped the question, and began to explain to Sheila what she advised her to do. In the meantime both the girls were to remain in her house. She would guarantee their being met by no one. When suitable rooms had been looked out by Paterson, they were to remove thither. The whole situation of affairs was at once perceived by Mrs. Lavender's attendant, who was given to understand that no one was to know of young Mrs. Lavender's being in the house. Then the old woman, much contented with what she had done, resolved that she would reward herself with a joke; and sent for Edward Ingram.

When Sheila, as already described, came into the room, and found her old friend there, the resolution she had formed went clean out of her mind. She forgot entirely the ban that had been placed on Ingram by her husband. But after her first emotion on seeing him was over, and when he began to discuss what she ought to do, and even to advise her in a diffident sort of way, she remembered all that she had forgotten, and was ashamed to find herself sitting there, and talking to him, as if it were in her father's house at Borva. Indeed, when he proposed to

take the management of her affairs into his own
hands, and to go and look at certain apartments
that Paterson had proposed, she was forced, with
great heart-burning and pain, to hint to him
that she could not avail herself of his kindness.

"But why?" he asked, with a stare of
surprise.

"You remember Brighton," she answered,
looking down. "You had a bad return for your
kindness to me then."

"Oh, I know," he said, carelessly. "And I
suppose Mr. Lavender wished you to cut me
after my impertinent interference. But things
are very much changed now. But for the time
he went North, he has been with me nearly
every hour since you left."

"Has Frank been to the Lewis?" she said,
suddenly, with a look of fear on her face.

"Oh no; he has only been to Glasgow to see
if you had gone to catch the *Clansman*, and go
North from there."

"Did he take the trouble to do all that?"
she asked, slowly and wistfully.

"Trouble!" cried Ingram. "He appears to
me neither to eat nor sleep day or night; but to
go wandering about in search of you in every
place where he fancies you may be. I never
saw a man so beside himself with anxiety——"

" I did not wish to make him anxious," said Sheila, in a low voice. " Will you tell him that I am well ? "

Mrs. Lavender began to smile. Were there not evident signs of softening ? But Ingram, who knew the girl better, was not deceived by these appearances. He could see that Sheila merely wished that her husband should not suffer pain on her account : that was all.

" I was about to ask you," he said, gently, " what I may say to him. He comes to me continually ; for he has always fancied that you would communicate with me. What shall I say to him, Sheila ? "

" You may tell him that I am well."

Mairi had by this time stepped out of the room. Sheila sat with her eyes fixed on the floor, her fingers working nervously with a paper-knife she held.

" Nothing more than that ? " he said.

" Nothing more."

He saw by her face, and he could tell by the sound of her voice, that her decision was resolute.

" Don't be a fool, child," said Mrs. Lavender, emphatically. " Here is your husband's friend, who can make everything straight and comfortable for you in an hour or two, and you quietly put aside the chance of reconciliation, and bring on yourself any amount of misery. I don't speak for Frank. Men can take care of themselves; they have clubs, and friends, and amusements for the whole day long. But you—what a pleasant life you would have, shut up in a couple of rooms, scarcely daring to show yourself at a window! Your fine sentiments are all very well; but they won't stand in the place of a husband to you; and you will soon find out the difference between living by yourself like that, and having some one in the house to look after you. Am I right, Mr. Ingram, or am I wrong?"

Ingram paused for a moment, and said—

"I have not the same courage that you have, Mrs. Lavender. I dare not advise Sheila one way or the other just at present. But if she feels in her own heart that she would rather return now to her husband, I can safely say that she would find him deeply grateful to her, and that he would try to do everything that she desired. That I know. He wants to see you, Sheila, if only for five minutes—to beg your forgiveness——"

"I cannot see him," she said, with the same sad and settled air.

"I am not to tell him where you are?"

"Oh no!" she cried, with a sudden and

startled emphasis. "You must not do that, Mr.
Ingram. Promise me you will not do that?"

"I do promise you; but you put a painful
duty on me, Sheila; for you know how he will
believe that a short interview with you would
put everything right, and he will look on me as
preventing that."

"Do you think a short interview at present
would put everything right?" she said, suddenly
looking up, and regarding him with her clear
and steadfast eyes.

He dared not answer. He felt in his inmost
heart that it would not.

"Ah, well," said Mrs. Lavender, "young
people have much satisfaction in being proud;
when they come to my age, they may find they
would have been happier if they had been less
disdainful."

"It is not disdain, Mrs. Lavender," said
Sheila, gently.

"Whatever it is," said the old woman, "I
must remind you two people that I am an in-
valid. Go away, and have luncheon. Paterson
will look after you. Mr. Ingram, give me that
book, that I may read myself into a nap; and
don't forget what I expect of you."

Ingram suddenly remembered. He and Sheila
and Mairi sat down to luncheon in the dining-

room; and, while he strove to get them to talk about Borva, he was thinking all the time of the extraordinary position he was expected to assume towards Sheila. Not only was he to be the repository of the secret of her place of residence, and the message-carrier between herself and her husband; but he was also to take Mrs. Lavender's fortune, in the event of her dying, and hold it in trust for the young wife. Surely this old woman, with her suspicious ways and her worldly wisdom, would not be so foolish as to hand him over all her property, free of conditions, on the simple understanding that when he chose he could give what he chose to Sheila? And yet that was what she had vowed she would do, to Ingram's profound dismay.

He laboured hard to lighten the spirits of those two girls. He talked of John the Piper, and said he would invite him up to London; and described his probable appearance in the Park. He told them stories of his adventures while he was camping out with some young artists in the western Highlands; and told them anecdotes, old, recent, and of his own invention, about the people he had met. Had they heard of the steward on board one of the Clyde steamers, who had a percentage on the drink consumed in the cabin, and who would call out

to the captain, "Why wass you going so fast?
Dinna put her into the quay so fast! There
is a gran' company down below, and they are
drinking fine!" Had he ever told them of the
porter at Arran who had demanded sixpence for
carrying up some luggage, but who, after being
sent to get a sovereign changed, came back with
only eighteen shillings, saying, "Oh, yes, it iss
sexpence! Oh, aye, it iss sexpence! But it iss
two shullens *ta you!*" Or of the other, who,
after being paid, hung about the cottage-door
for nearly an hour, until Ingram, coming out,
asked him why he had waited; whereupon he
said, with an air of perfect indifference, "Oo aye,
there wass something said about a dram; but
hoot toots! it is of no consequence whatever!"
And was it true that the Sheriff of Stornoway
was so kind-hearted a man that he remitted the
punishment of certain culprits, ordained by the
statute to be whipped with birch-rods, on the
ground that the island of Lewis produced no
birch, and that he was not bound to import it?
And had Mairi heard any more of the Black
Horse of Loch Suainabhal? And where had
she pulled those splendid bunches of bell-
heather?

He suddenly stopped, and Sheila looked up
with inquiring eyes. How did he know that

Mairi had brought those things with her? Sheila saw that he must have gone up with her husband, and must have seen the room which she had decorated in imitation of the small parlour at Borvabost. She would rather not think of that room now.

"When are you going to the Lewis?" she asked of him, with her eyes cast down.

"Well, I think I have changed my mind about that, Sheila. I don't think I shall go to the Lewis this autumn."

Her face became more and more embarrassed; how was she to thank him for his continued thoughtfulness and self-sacrifice?

"There is no necessity," he said, lightly. "The man I am going with has no particular purpose in view. We shall merely go cruising about those wonderful lochs and islands; and I am sure to run against some of those young fellows I know, who are prowling about the fishing-villages with portable easels. They are good boys, those boys. They are very hospitable, if they have only a single bed-room in a small cottage as their studio and reception-room combined. I should not wonder, Sheila, if I went ashore somewhere, and put up my lot with those young fellows, and listened to their wicked stories, and live on whisky and herrings for a

month. Would you like to see me return to
Whitehall in kilts? And I should go into the
office, and salute everybody with 'And are you
ferry well?' just as Mairi does. But don't be
down-hearted, Mairi. You speak English a good
deal better than many English folks I know;
and by the time you go back to the Lewis, we
shall have you fit to become a school-mistress,
not only in Borva, but in Stornoway itself."

"I wass told it is ferry good English they
hef in Stornoway," said Mairi, not very sure
whether Mr. Ingram was joking or not.

"My dear child!" he cried, "I tell you it is
the best English in the world. If the Queen
only knew, she would send her grandchildren to
be educated there. But I must go now. Good-
bye, Mairi. I mean to come and take you to a
theatre some night soon."

Sheila accompanied him out into the hall.

"When shall you see him?" she said, with
her eyes cast down.

"This evening," he answered.

"I should like you to tell him that I am well,
and that he need not be anxious about me."

"And that is all?"

"Yes, that is all."

"Very well, Sheila. I wish you had given
me a pleasanter message to carry; but when

you think of doing that, I shall be glad to take it."

"Ingram left, and hastened in to his office. Sheila's affairs were considerably interfering with his attendance there, there could be no question of that; but he had the reputation of being able to get through his work thoroughly, whatever might be the hours he devoted to it; so that he did not greatly fear being rebuked for his present irregularities. Perhaps, if a grave official warning had been probable, even that would not have interfered much with his determination to do what could be done for Sheila.

But this business of carrying a message to Lavender was the most serious he had as yet undertaken. He had to make sundry and solemn resolves to put a bold face on the matter at the outset, and declare that wild horses would not tear from him any further information. He feared the piteous appeals that might be made to him; the representations that, merely for the sake of an imprudent promise, he was delaying a reconciliation between these two until that might be impossible; the reasons that would be urged on him for considering Sheila's welfare as paramount to his own scruples. He went through the interview, as he foresaw it, a dozen times over; and constructed replies to each

argument and entreaty. Of course it would be
simple enough to meet all Lavender's demands
with a simple "No;" but there are circumstances in which the heroic method of solving
difficulties becomes a trifle inhuman.

He had promised to dine with Lavender that
evening at his club. When he went along to
St. James's Street at the appointed hour, his
host had not arrived. He walked about for ten
minutes, and then Lavender appeared, haggard
and worn-out with fatigue.

"I have heard nothing—I can hear nothing
—I have been everywhere," he said, leading the
way at once into the dining-room. "I am sorry
I have kept you waiting, Ingram."

They sat down at a small side-table; there
were few men in the club at this late season; so
that they could talk freely enough when the
waiter had come and gone.

"Well, I have some news for you, Lavender,"
Ingram said.

"Do you know where she is?" said the other,
eagerly.

"Yes."

"Where?" he almost called aloud, in his
anxiety.

"Well," Ingram said, slowly, "she is in London, and she is very well; and you need have
no anxiety about her."

"But where is she?" demanded Lavender, taking no heed of the waiter who was standing by and uncorking a bottle.

"I promised her not to tell you."

"You have spoken with her, then?"

"Yes."

"What did she say? Where has she been? Good heavens, Ingram! you don't mean to say you are going to keep it a secret?"

"Oh no," said the other; "I will tell you everything she said to me, if you like. Only I will not tell you where she is——."

"I will not ask you," said Lavender, at once, "if she does not wish me to know. But you can tell me about herself. What did she say? What was she looking like? Is Mairi with her?"

"Yes, Mairi is with her. And of course she is looking a little troubled, and pale, and so forth; but she is very well, I should think, and quite comfortably situated. She said I was to tell you that she was well, and that you need not be anxious."

"She sent a message to me?"

"That is it."

"By Jove, Ingram! how can I ever thank you enough? I feel as glad just now as if she had really come home again. And how did you manage it?"

Lavender, in his excitement and gratitude, kept filling up his friend's glass the moment the least quantity had been taken out of it; the wonder was he did not fill all the glasses on that side of the table, and beseech Ingram to have two or three dinners all at once.

"Oh, you needn't give me any credit about it," Ingram said. "I stumbled against her by accident— t least, I did not find her out myself."

"Did she send for you?"

"No. But look here, Lavender, this sort of cross-examination will lead to but one thing; and you say yourself you won't try to find out where she is."

"Not from you, anyway. But how can I help wanting to know where she is? And my aunt was saying just now that very likely she had gone right away to the other end of London —to Peckham, or some such place."

"You have seen Mrs. Lavender, then?"

"I have just come from there. The old heathen thinks the whole affair rather a good joke; but perhaps that was only her way of showing her temper, for she was in a bit of a rage, to be sure. And so Sheila sent me that message?"

"Yes."

"Does she want money? Would you take

her some money from me?" he said eagerly. Any bond of union between him and Sheila would be of some value.

"I don't think she needs money; and in any case, I know she wouldn't take it from you."

"Well, now, Ingram, you have seen her, and talked with her. What do you think she intends to do? What do you think she would have me do?"

"These are very dangerous questions for me to answer," Ingram said. "I don't see how you can expect me to assume the responsibility."

"I don't ask you to do that at all. But I never found your advice to fail. And if you give me any hint as to what I should do, I will do it on my own responsibility."

"Then I won't. But this I will do. I will tell you as nearly as ever I can what she said; and you can judge for yourself."

Very cautiously indeed did Ingram set out on this perilous undertaking. It was no easy matter so to shut out all references to Sheila's surroundings, that no hint should be given to this anxious listener as to her whereabouts. But Ingram got through it successfully; and when he had finished, Lavender sat some time in silence, merely toying with his knife, for, indeed, he had eaten nothing.

"If it is her wish," he said, slowly, "that I should not go to see her, I will not try to do so. But I should like to know where she is. You say she is comfortable, and she has Mairi for a companion—and that is something. In the meantime, I suppose I must wait."

"I don't see myself how waiting is likely to do much good," said Ingram. "That won't alter your relations much."

"It may alter her determination. A woman is sure to soften into charity and forgiveness. She can't help it."

"If you were to ask Sheila now, she would say she had forgiven you already. But that is a different matter from getting her to resume her former method of life with you. To tell you the truth, I should strongly advise her, if I were to give advice at all, not to attempt anything of the sort. One failure is bad enough, and has wrought sufficient trouble.

"Then what am I to do, Ingram?"

"You must judge for yourself what is the most likely way of winning back Sheila's confidence in you, and the most likely conditions under which she might be induced to join you again. You need not expect to get her back into that Square, I should fancy; *that* experiment has rather broken down."

"Well," said Lavender, "I shan't bore you

any more just now about my affairs. Look after your dinner, old fellow; your starving yourself won't help me much."

"I don't mean to starve myself at all," said Ingram, steadily making his way through the abundant dishes his friend had ordered. "But I had a very good luncheon this morning with——"

"With Sheila," Lavender said, quickly.

"Yes. Does it surprise you to find that she is in a place where she can get food? I wish the poor child had made better use of her opportunities."

"Ingram," he said, after a minute, "could you take some money from me, without her knowing of it, and try to get her some of the little things she likes—some delicacies, you know—they might be smuggled in, as it were, without her knowing who had paid for them? There was ice-pudding, you know, with straw-berries in it, that she was fond of——"

"My dear fellow, a woman in her position thinks of something else than ice-pudding in strawberries——"

"But why shouldn't she have it all the same? I would give twenty pounds to get some little gratification of that sort conveyed to her; and if you could try, Ingram——"

"My dear fellow, she has got everything she can want: there was no ice-pudding at luncheon, but doubtless there will be at dinner."

So Sheila was staying in a house in which ices could be prepared? Lavender's suggestion had had no cunning intention in it; but here was an obvious piece of information. She was in no humble lodging-house, then. She was either staying with some friends—and she had no friends but Lavender's friends—or she was staying at an hotel. He remembered that she had once dined at the Langham, Mrs. Kavanagh having persuaded her to go to meet some American visitors. Might she have gone thither?

Lavender was somewhat silent during the rest of that meal; for he was thinking of other things besides the mere question as to where Sheila might be staying. He was trying to imagine what she may have felt before she was driven to this step. He was trying to recall all manner of incidents of their daily life that he now saw might have appeared to her in a very different light from that in which he saw them. He was wondering, too, how all this could be altered; and a new life began for them both, if that were still possible.

They had gone up-stairs into the smoking-room, when a card was brought to Lavender.

"Young Mosenberg is below," he said to Ingram. "He will be a livelier companion for you than I could be. Waiter, ask this gentleman to come up."

The handsome Jew-boy came eagerly into the room, with much excitement visible on his face.

"Oh, do you know," he said to Lavender, "I have found out where Mrs. Lavender is, yes: she is at your aunt's house. I saw her this afternoon—for one moment——"

He stopped; for he saw by the vexation on Ingram's face that he had done something wrong.

"Is it a mistake?" he said. "Is it a secret?"

"It is not likely to be a secret if you have got hold of it," said Ingram, sharply.

"I am very sorry," said the boy. "I thought you were all anxious to know——"

"It does not matter in the least," said Lavender, quietly, to both of them. "I shall not seek to disturb her. I am about to leave London."

"Where are you going," said the boy.

"I don't know yet."

That, at least, had been part of the result of his meditations; and Ingram, looking at him, wondered whether he meant to go away without trying to say one word to Sheila.

" Look here, Lavender," he said, " you must not fancy we were trying to play any useless and impertinent trick. To-morrow or next day Sheila will leave your aunt's house; and then I should have told you she had been there, and how the old lady received her. It was Sheila's own wish that the lodgings she is going to should not be known. She fancies that would save both of you a great deal of unnecessary and fruitless pain, do you see. That really is her only object in wishing to have any conceal-ment about the matter."

" But there is no need for any such conceal-ment," he said. " You may tell Sheila that if she likes to stay on with my aunt, so much the better; and I take it very kind of her that she went there, instead of going home, or to a strange house."

" Am I to tell her that you mean to leave London ? "

" Yes."

They went into the billiard-room. Mosen-berg was not permitted to play, as he had not dined in the club; but Ingram and Lavender proceeded to have a game, the former being content to accept something like thirty in a hundred. It was speedily very clear that Lavender's heart was not in the contest. He

kept forgetting which ball he had been playing;
missing easy shots; playing a perversely wrong
game; and so forth. And yet his spirits were
not much downcast.

"Is Peter Hewetson still at Tarbert, do you
know?" he asked of Ingram.

"I believe so. I heard of him lately. He
and one or two more are there."

"I suppose you'll look in on them if you go
North?"

"Certain. The place is badly perfumed, but
picturesque; and there is generally plenty of
whisky about."

"When do you go North?"

"I don't know. In a week or two."

That was all that Lavender hinted of his
plans. He went home early that night, and
spent an hour or two in packing up some things,
and in writing a long letter to his aunt, which
was destined considerably to astonish that lady.
Then he lay down, and had a few hours' rest.

In the early morning he went out and walked
across Kensington Gardens down to the Gore.
He wished to have one look at the house in
which Sheila was; or perhaps he might, from a
distance, see her come out on a simple errand?
He knew, for example, that she had a super-
stitious liking for posting her letters herself; in

wet weather or dry, she invariably carried her
own correspondence to the nearest pillar-post.
Perhaps he might have one glimpse of her face,
to see how she was looking, before he left
London.

There were few people about; one or two
well-known lawyers and merchants were riding
by to have their morning canter in the Park;
the shops were being opened. Over there was
the house—with its dark front of bricks, its hard
ivy, and its small windows with formal red curtains—in which Sheila was immured. That was
certainly not the palace that a beautiful Sea-
Princess should have inhabited. Where were
the pine woods around it, and the lofty hills,
and the wild beating of the waves on the sands
below? And now it seemed strange and sad
that just as he was about to go away to the
North, and breathe the salt air again, and find
the strong west winds blowing across the mountain peaks and through the furze, Sheila, a
daughter of the sea and the rocks, should be
hiding herself in obscure lodgings in the heart
of a great city. Perhaps—he could not but
think at this time—if he had only the chance of
speaking to her for a couple of moments he
could persuade her to forgive him everything
that had happened, and go away with him—

away from London and all the associations that
had vexed her and almost broke her heart—to
the free, and open, and joyous life on the far
sea-coasts of the Hebrides.

Something caused him to turn his head for a
second, and he knew that Sheila was coming
along the pavement, not from, but towards the
house. It was too late to think of getting out
of her way; and yet he dared not go up to her
and speak to her, as he had wished to do.
She, too, had seen him. There was a quick,
frightened look in her eyes; and then she came
along, with her face pale, and her head downcast. He did not seek to interrupt her. His
eyes, too, were lowered as she passed him without taking any notice of his presence, although
the sad face and the troubled lips told of the
pain at her heart. He had hoped, perchance,
for one word, for even a sign of recognition;
but she went by him calmly, gravely, and
silently. She went into the house; and he
turned away, with a weight at his heart, as
though the gates of heaven had been closed
against him.

CHAPTER IV.

"LIKE HADRIANUS AND AUGUSTUS."

THE island of Borva lay warm, and green, and bright under a blue sky; there were no white curls of foam on Loch Roag, but only the long Atlantic swell coming in to fall on the white beach; away over there in the south the fine greys and purples of the giant Suainabhal shone in the sunlight amid the clear air; and the beautiful seapyots flew about the rocks, their screaming being the only sound audible in the stillness. The King of Borva was down by the shore, seated on a stool, and engaged in the idyllic operation of painting a boat which had been hauled up on the sand. It was the *Maigh-dean-mhara.* He would let no one else on the island touch Sheila's boat. Duncan, it is true, was permitted to keep her masts and sails and seats sound and white; but as for the decorative painting of the small craft—including a little bit of amateur gilding—that was the exclusive right of Mr. Mackenzie himself. For of course, the old man said to himself, Sheila was coming back to Borva one of these days; and she would be proud to find her own boat bright and sound. If she and her husband should resolve to spend half the year in Stornoway, would not the small craft be of use to her there, and sure he was that a prettier little vessel never entered Stornoway bay. Mr. Mackenzie was at this moment engaged in putting a thin line of green round the white bulwarks that might have been distinguished across Loch Roag, so keen and pure was the colour.

A much heavier boat, broad-beamed, red-hulled, and brown-sailed, was slowly coming round the point at this moment. Mr. Mackenzie raised his eyes from his work, and knew that Duncan was coming back from Callernish. Some few minutes thereafter, the boat was run in to her moorings, and Duncan came along the beach with a parcel in his hand.

"Here wass your letters, sir," he said. "And there iss one of them will be from Miss Sheila, if I wass make no mistake."

He remained there. Duncan generally knew pretty well when a letter from Sheila was among the documents he had to deliver; and, on such

an occasion, he invariably lingered about to hear
the news, which was immediately spread abroad
throughout the island. The old King of Borva
was not a garrulous man; but he was glad that
the people about him should know that his
Sheila had become a fine lady in the south, and
saw fine things, and went among fine people.
Perhaps this notion of his was a sort of apology
to them—perhaps it was an apology to himself
—for his having let her go away from the island;
but at all events the simple folks about Borva
knew that Miss Sheila, as they still invariably
called her, lived in the same town as the Queen
herself, and saw many lords and ladies, and was
present at great festivities, as became Mr. Mackenzie's only daughter. And naturally these
rumours and stories were exaggerated by the
kindly interest and affection of the people into
something far beyond what Sheila's father intended; insomuch that many an old crone would
proudly and sagaciously wag her head, and say
that when Miss Sheila came back to Borva
strange things might be seen, and it would be
a proud day for Mr. Mackenzie if he was to
go down to the shore to meet Queen Victoria
herself, and the Princes and Princesses, and
many fine people, all come to stay at his house
and have great rejoicings in Borva.

Thus it was that Duncan invariably lingered about when he brought a letter from Sheila; and if her father happened to forget, or be pre-occupied, Duncan would humbly but firmly remind him. On this occasion Mr. Mackenzie put down his paint-brush and took the bundle of letters and newspapers Duncan had brought him. He selected that from Sheila, and threw the others on the beach beside him.

There was really no news in the letter. Sheila merely said that she could not as yet answer her father's question as to the time she might probably visit Lewis. She hoped he was well; and that, if she could not get up to Borva that year, he would come south to London for a time, when the hard weather set in in the north. And so forth. But there was something in the tone of the letter that struck the old man as being unusual and strange. It was very formal in its phraseology. He read it twice over, very carefully, and forgot altogether that Duncan was waiting. Indeed, he was going to turn away, forgetting his work and the other letters that still lay on the beach, when he observed that there was a postscript on the other side of the last page. It merely said—" *Will you please address your letters now to No. — Pembroke Road, South Kensington, where I may be for some time?*"

That was an imprudent postscript. If she had shown the letter to anyone, she would have been warned of the blunder she was committing. But the child had not much cunning; and wrote and posted the letter in the belief that her father would simply do as she asked him, and suspect nothing, and ask no questions.

When old Mackenzie read that postscript, he could only stare at the paper before him.

"Will there be anything wrong, sir?" said the tall keeper, whose keen grey eyes had been fixed on his master's face.

The sound of Duncan's voice startled and re-called Mr. Mackenzie, who immediately turned, and said, lightly—

"Wrong? What wass you thinking would be wrong? Oh, there is nothing wrong what-ever. But Mairi, she will be greatly surprised, and she is going to write no letters until she comes back to tell you what she has seen; that is the message there will be for Scarlett. Sheila —she is very well."

Duncan picked up the other letters and news-papers.

"You may tek them to the house, Duncan," said Mr. Mackenzie, and then he added, care-lessly, "Did you hear when the steamer was thinking of leaving Stornoway this night?"

"They were saying it would be seven o'clock or six, as there was a great deal of cargo to go on her."

"Six o'clock? I'm thinking, Duncan, I would like to go with her as far as Oban or Glasgow. Oh yes, I will go with her as far as Glasgow. Be sharp, Duncan, and bring in the boat."

The keeper stared, fearing his master had gone mad.

"You wass going with her this ferry night?"

"Yes. Be sharp, Duncan!" said Mackenzie, doing his best to conceal his impatience and determination under a careless air.

"Bit, sir, you canna do it," said Duncan, peevishly. "You hef no things looked out to go. And by the time we would get to Callernish, it wass a ferry hard drive there will be to get to Stornoway by six o'clock; and there is the mare, sir, she will hef lost a shoe——"

Mr. Mackenzie's diplomacy gave way. He turned upon the keeper with a sudden fierceness, and with a stamp of his foot.

"————you, Duncan MacDonald, is it you or me that is the master? I will go to Stornoway this ferry moment if I hef to buy twenty horses!" And there was a light under the shaggy eyebrows that warned Duncan to have done with his remonstrances.

"Oh, ferry well, sir—ferry well, sir," he said, going off to the boat, and grumbling as he went. "If Miss Sheila wass here, it would be no going away to Glesca without any things wis you, as if you wass a poor traffelin tailor that hass nothing in the world but a needle and a thimble mirover. And what will the people in Styornoway hef to say, and sa captain of sa steamboat; and Scarlett—I will hef no peace from Scarlett if you wass going away like this. And as for sa sweerin, it is no use sa sweerin, for I will get sa boat ready—oh yes, I will get the boat ready—but I do not understand why I will get sa boat ready."

By this time, indeed, he had got along to the larger boat, and his grumblings were inaudible to the object of them. Mr. Mackenzie went to the small landing-place, and waited. When he got into the boat, and sat down in the stern, taking the tiller in his right hand, he still held Sheila's letter in the other hand, although he did not need to re-read it.

They sailed out into the blue waters of the loch, and rounded the point of the island, in absolute silence, Duncan meanwhile being both sulky and curious. He could not make out why his master should so suddenly leave the island, without informing anyone, without even taking with him that tall and roughly-furred black hat which he ordinarily wore on important occasions. Yet there was a letter in his hand; and it was a letter from Miss Sheila. Was the news about Mairi the only news in it?

Duncan kept looking ahead to see that the boat was steering her right course for the Narrows, and was anxious, now that he had started, to make the voyage in the least possible time; but all the same his eyes would come back to Mr. Mackenzie, who sat very much absorbed, steering almost mechanically, seldom looking ahead, but instinctively guessing his course by the outlines of the shore close by.

"Wass there any bad news, sir, from Miss Sheila?" he was compelled to say at last.

"Miss Sheila!" said Mr. Mackenzie, impatiently. "Is it an infant you are, that you will call a married woman by such a name?"

Duncan had never been checked before for a habit which was common to the whole island of Borva.

"There iss no bad news," continued Mackenzie, impatiently. "Is it a story you would like to tek back to the people of Borvabost?"

"It was no thought of such a thing wass come into my head, sir," said Duncan. "There is no one in sa island would like to carry bad news about Miss Sheila; and there iss no one in sa island would like to hear it—not anyone whatever; and I can answer for that."

"Then hold your tongue about it—there is no bad news from Sheila," said Mackenzie; and Duncan relapsed into silence, not very well content.

By dint of very hard driving indeed Mr. Mackenzie just caught the boat as she was leaving Stornoway harbour; the hurry he was in fortunately saving him from the curiosity and inquiries of the people he knew on the pier. As for the frank and good-natured captain, he did not show that excessive interest in Mr. Mackenzie's affairs that Duncan had feared; but when the steamer was well away from the coast, and bearing down on her route to Skye, he came and had a chat with the King of Borva about the condition of affairs on the west of the island, and he was good enough to ask, too, about the young lady who had married the English gentleman. Mr. Mackenzie said briefly that she was very well; and returned to the subject of the fishing.

It was on a wet and dreary morning that Mr. Mackenzie arrived in London; and as he was slowly driven through the long and dismal thoroughfares, with their grey and melancholy houses, their passers-by under umbrellas, and their smoke, and drizzle, and dirt, he could not help saying to himself, "My poor Sheila!" It was not a pleasant place surely to live in always, although it might be all very well for a visit. Indeed, this cheerless day added to the gloomy forebodings in his mind;. and it needed all his resolve, and his pride in his own diplomacy, to carry out his plan of approaching Sheila.

When he got to Pembroke Road, he stopped the cab at the corner, and paid the man. Then he walked along the thoroughfare, having a look at the houses. At length he came to the number mentioned in Sheila's letter, and he found that there was a brass plate on the door bearing an unfamiliar name. His suspicions were confirmed. He went up the steps and knocked; a small girl answered the summons.

"Is Mrs. Lavender living here?" he said.

She looked for a moment with some surprise at the short, thick-set man, with his sailor costume, his peaked cap, and his great grey beard and shaggy eyebrows ; and then she said that she would ask, and what was his name? But Mr. Mackenzie was too sharp not to know what that meant.

"I am her father. It will do ferry well if you will show me the room."

And he stepped inside. The small girl obediently shut the door, and then led the way upstairs. The next minute Mr. Mackenzie had entered the room, and there, before him, was Sheila, bending over Mairi, and teaching her how to do some fancy-work.

The girl looked up, on hearing some one enter, and then, when she suddenly saw her father there, she uttered a slight cry of alarm, and shrunk back. If he had been less intent on his own plans, he would have been amazed and pained by this action on the part of his daughter, who used to run to him, on great occasions and small, whenever she saw him; but the girl had for the last few days been so habitually schooling herself into the notion that she was keeping a secret from him—she had become so deeply conscious of the concealment intended in that brief letter—that she instinctively shrank from him when he suddenly appeared. It was but for a moment. Mr. Mackenzie came forward, with a fine assumption of carelessness, and shook hands with Sheila and with Mairi, and said—

"How do you do, Mairi? And are you ferry well, Sheila? And you will not expect me this morning; but when a man will not pay you what he wass owing, it was no good letting it go on in that way, and I hef come to London——"

He shook the rain-drops from his cap, and was a little embarrassed.

"Yes, I hef come to London to have an account settled up; for it wass no good letting the man go on for effer and effer. Ay, and how are you, Sheila?"

He glanced about the room—he would not look at her. She stood there, unable to speak, and with her face grown wild and pale.

"Ay, it wass raining hard all the last night, and there was a good deal of water came into the carriage; and it is a ferry hard bed you will make of a third-class carriage. Ay, it wass so. And this is a new house you will hef, Sheila——"

She had been coming nearer to him, with her face down, and the speechless lips trembling. And then suddenly, with a strange sob, she threw herself into his arms, and hid her head, and burst into a wild fit of crying.

"Sheila," he said, "what ails you? What iss all the matter?"

Mairi had covertly got out of the room.

"Oh, papa, I have left him," the girl cried.

"Ay," said her father, quite cheerfully, "oh ay, I thought there was some little thing wrong

when your letter wass come to us the other day.
But it is no use making a great deal of trouble
about it, Sheila; for it is easy to have all those
things put right again—oh yes, ferry easy. And
you hef left your own home, Sheila? And
where is Mr. Lavender?"

"Oh, papa," she cried, " you must not try to
see him. You must promise not to go to see him. I
should have told you everything when I wrote, but
I thought you would come up, and blame it all on
him, and I think it is I who am to blame——"

" But I do not want to blame anyone," said
her father. " You must not make so much of
these things, Sheila. It is a pity—yes, it is a
ferry great pity—your husband and you will hef
a quarrel; but it iss no uncommon thing for
these troubles to happen; and I am coming to
you this morning, not to make any more trouble,
but to see if it cannot be put right· again. And
I do not want to know any more than that; and
I will not blame anyone; but if I wass to see
Mr. Lavender——"

A bitter anger had filled his heart from the
moment he had learned how matters stood; and
yet he was talking in such a bland, matter-of-
fact, almost cheerful fashion, that his own
daughter was imposed upon, and began to grow
comforted. The mere fact that her father now

knew of all her troubles, and was not disposed
to take a very gloomy view of them, was of itself
a great relief to her. And she was greatly
pleased, too, to hear her father talk in the same
light and even friendly fashion of her husband.
She had dreaded the possible results of her
writing home and relating what had occurred.
She knew the powerful passion of which this
lonely old man was capable ; and if he had come
suddenly down south, with a wild desire to
revenge the wrongs of his daughter, what might
not have happened?

Sheila sat down, and with averted eyes told
her father the whole story, ingenuously making
all possible excuses for her husband, and intimat-
ing strongly that the more she looked over the
history of the past time, the more she was
convinced that she was herself to blame. It was
but natural that Mr. Lavender should like to
live in the manner to which he had been accustomed. She had tried to live that way, too ;
and the failure to do so was surely her fault.
He had been very kind to her. He was always
buying her new dresses, jewellery, and what
not ; and was always pleased to take her to be
amused anywhere. All this she said, and a great
deal more ; and although Mr. Mackenzie did not
believe the half of it, he did not say so.

" Ay, ay, Sheila," he said, cheerfully, " but if everything was right like that, what for will you be here ? "

" But everything was not right, papa," the girl said, still with her eyes cast down. " I could not live any longer like that ; and I had to come away. That is my fault ; and I could not help it. And there was a—a misunderstanding between us about Mairi's visit—for I had said nothing about it__and he was surprised—and he had some friends coming to see us that day——"

" Oh, well, there iss no great harm done— none at all," said her father lightly, and perhaps beginning to think that after all something was to be said on Lavender's side of the question. " And you will not suppose, Sheila, that I am coming to make any trouble by quarrelling with anyone. There are some men—oh yes, there are ferry many—that would hef no judgment at such a time, and they would think only about their daughter, and hef no regard for anyone else, and they would only make effery one angrier than before. But you will tell me, Sheila, where Mr. Lavender is——"

" I do not know," she said. " And I am anxious, papa, you should not go to see him. I have asked you to promise that to please me."

He hesitated. There were not many things he

could refuse his daughter; but he was not sure he ought to yield to her in this. For where not these two a couple of foolish young things, who wanted an experienced, and cool, and shrewd person to come with a little dexterous management and arrange their affairs for them?

"I do not think I have half explained the difference between us," said Sheila, in the same low voice. "It is no passing quarrel to be mended up and forgotten—it is nothing like that. You must leave it alone, papa."

"That is foolishness, Sheila," said the old man, with a little impatience. "You are making big things out of ferry little; and you will only bring trouble to yourself. How do you know but that he wishes to hef all this misunderstanding removed, and hef you go back to him?"

"I know that he wishes that," she said, calmly.

"And you speak as if you wass in great trouble here, and yet you will not go back?" he said, in great surprise.

"Yes, that is so," she said. "There is no use in my going back to the same sort of life: it was not happiness for either of us—and to me it was misery. If I am to blame for it, that is only a misfortune."

"But if you will not go back to him, Sheila,"

her father said, "at least you will go back with me to Borva."

"I cannot do that either," said the girl, with the same quiet yet decisive manner.

Mr. Mackenzie rose, with an impatient gesture, and walked to the window. He did not know what to say. He was very well aware that when Sheila had resolved upon anything, she had thought it well over beforehand, and was not likely to change her mind. And yet the notion of his daughter living in lodgings in a strange town—her only companion a young girl who had never been in the place before—was vexatiously absurd.

"Sheila," he said, "you will come to a better understanding about that. I suppose you wass afraid the people would wonder at your coming back alone. But they will know nothing about it. Mairi she is a ferry good lass; she will do anything you will ask of her; you hef no need to think she will carry stories. And everyone wass thinking you will be coming to the Lewis this year, and it is ferry glad they will be to see you; and if the house at Borvabost has not enough amusement for you, after you hef been in a big town like this, you will live in Stornoway with some of our friends there, and you will come over to Borva when you please."

"If I went up to the Lewis," said Sheila, "do you think I could live anywhere but in Borva? It is not any amusements I will be thinking about. But I cannot go back to the Lewis alone."

Her father saw how the pride of the girl had driven her to this decision; and saw, too, how useless it was for him to reason with her just at the present moment. Still there was plenty of occasion here for the use of a little diplomacy, merely to smooth the way for the reconciliation of husband and wife; and Mr. Mackenzie concluded in his own mind that it was far from injudicious to allow Sheila to convince herself that she bore part of the blame of this separation. For example, he now proposed that the discussion of the whole question should be postponed for the present; and that Sheila should take him about London and show him all that she had learned; and he suggested that they should then and there get a hansom cab and drive to some exhibition or other.

"A hansom, papa?" said Sheila. "Mairi must go with us, you know."

This was precisely what he had angled for; and he said, with a show of impatience—

"Mairi; how can we take about Mairi to every place? Mairi is a ferry good lass—oh, yes—but she is a servant-lass."

The words nearly stuck in his throat; and, indeed, had any other addressed such a phrase to one of his kith and kin there would have been an explosion of rage; but now he was determined to show to Sheila that her husband had some cause for objecting to this girl sitting down with his friends.

But neither husband nor father could make Sheila forswear allegiance to what her own heart told her was just, and honourable, and generous; and indeed her father at this moment was not displeased to see her turn round on himself. with just a touch of indignation in her voice.

"Mairi is my guest, papa," she said. "It is not like you to think of leaving her at home."

"Oh, it wass of no consequence," said old Mackenzie, carelessly—indeed he was not sorry to have met with this rebuff. "Mairi is a ferry good girl—oh, yes—but there are many who would not forget she is a servant-lass, and would not like to be always taking her with them. And you hef lived a long time in London——"

"I have not lived long enough in London to make me forget my friends, or insult them," Sheila said, with proud lips, and yet turning to the window to hide her face.

"My lass, I did not mean any harm whatever," her father said, gently; "I was saying

nothing against Mairi. Go away and bring her
into the room, Sheila; and we will see what we
can do now, and if there is a theatre we can go
to this evening. And I must go out, too, to
buy some things; for you are a ferry fine lady
now, Sheila, and I was coming away in such a
hurry——"

"Where is your luggage, papa?" she said,
suddenly.

"Oh, luggage?" said Mackenzie, looking
round in great embarrassment. "It wass luggage you said, Sheila? Ay, well, it wass a
hurry I wass in when I came away—for this
man he will hef to pay me at once whatever—
and there was no time for any luggage—oh no,
there wass no time, because Duncan he wass
late with the boat, and the mare she had a shoe
to put on—and—and—oh no, there wass no
time for any luggage."

"But what was Scarlett about, to let you
come away like that?" Sheila said.

"Scarlett? Well, Scarlett did not know—
it was all in such a hurry. Now go and bring
in Mairi, Sheila; and we will speak about the
theatre."

But there was to be no theatre for any of
them that evening. Sheila was just about to
leave the room to summon Mairi, when the

small girl who had let Mackenzie into the house appeared and said—

" Please m'm, there is a young woman below who wishes to see you. She has a message to you from Mrs. Paterson."

" Mrs. Paterson ? " Sheila said, wondering how Mrs. Lavender's hench-woman should have been entrusted with any such commission. " Will you ask her to come up ? "

The girl came up stairs, looking rather frightened, and much out of breath.

" Please m'm, Mrs. Paterson has sent me to tell you, and would you please come as soon as it is convenient. Mrs. Lavender has died. It was quite sudden—only she recovered a little after the fit, and then sank ; the doctor is there now ; but he wasn't in time, it was all so sudden. Will you please come round, m'm ? "

" Yes—I shall be there directly," said Sheila, too bewildered and stunned to think of the possibility of meeting her husband there.

The girl left ; and Sheila still stood in the middle of the room apparently stupefied. That old woman had got into such a habit of talking about her approaching death that Sheila had ceased to believe her, and had grown to fancy that these morbid speculations were indulged in chiefly for the sake of shocking bystanders.

But a dead man or a dead woman is suddenly invested with a great solemnity; and Sheila, with a pang of remorse, thought of the fashion in which she had suspected this old woman of a godless hypocrisy. She felt, too, that she had unjustly disliked Mrs. Lavender—that she had feared to go near her, and blamed her unfairly for many things that had happened. In her own way that old woman in Kensington Gore had been kind to her; perhaps the girl was a little ashamed of herself at this moment that she did not cry.

Her father went out with her and up to the house with the dusty ivy and the red curtains. How strangely like was the aspect of the house inside to the very picture that Mrs. Lavender had herself drawn of her death. Sheila could remember all the ghastly details that the old woman seemed to have a malicious delight in describing, and here they were—the shutters drawn down, the servants walking about on tiptoe, the strange silence in one particular room. The little shrivelled old body lay quite still and calm now; and yet as Sheila went to the bedside, she could hardly believe that within that forehead there was not some consciousness of the scene around. Lying almost in the same position the old woman,

with a sardonic smile on her face, had spoken of
the time when she should be speechless, sight-
less, and deaf, while Paterson would go about
stealthily as if she was afraid the corpse would
hear. Was it possible to believe that the dead
body was not conscious at this moment that
Paterson was really going about in that fashion
—that the blinds were down, friends standing
some little distance from the bed, a couple of
doctors talking to each other in the passage
outside?

They went into another room, and then
Sheila, with a sudden shiver, remembered that
soon her husband would be coming, and might
meet her and her father there.

"You have sent for Mr. Lavender?" she said,
calmly, to Mrs. Paterson.

"No, ma'am," Paterson said, with more than
her ordinary gravity and formality. "I did not
know where to send for him. He left London
some days ago. Perhaps you would read the
letter, ma'am."

She offered Sheila an open letter. The girl
saw that it was in her husband's handwriting;
but she shrank from it as though she were
violating the secrets of the grave.

"Oh no," she said, "I cannot do that."

"Mrs. Lavender, ma'am, meant you to read

it, after she had had her will altered. She told
me so. It is a very sad thing, ma'am, that she
did not live to carry out her intentions; for she
has been inquiring, ma'am, these last few days
as to how she could leave everything to you,
ma'am, which she intended, and now the other
will——"

"Oh, don't talk about that!" said Sheila.
It seemed to her that the dead body in the other
room would be laughing hideously, if only it
could, at this fulfilment of all the sardonic pro-
phecies that Mrs. Lavender used to make.

"I beg your pardon, ma'am," Paterson said,
in the same formal way, as if she were a
machine set to work in a particular direction,
"I only mentioned the will to explain why Mrs.
Lavender wished you to read this letter."

"Read the letter, Sheila," said her father.

The girl took it and carried it to the window.
While she was there, old Mackenzie, who had
fewer scruples about such matters, and who had
the curiosity natural to a man of the world, said
to Mrs. Paterson—not loud enough for Sheila
to overhear—

"I suppose, then, the poor old lady has left
her property to her nephew?"

"Oh no, sir," said Mrs. Paterson, somewhat
sadly, for she fancied she was the bearer of bad

news. "She had a will drawn out only a short time ago, and nearly everything is left to Mr. Ingram."

"To Mr. Ingram?"

"Yes," said the woman, amazed to see that Mackenzie's face, so far from evincing displeasure, seemed to be as delighted as it was surprised.

"Yes, sir," said Mrs. Paterson, "I was one of the witnesses. But Mrs. Lavender changed her mind; and was very anxious that everything should go to your daughter, if it could be done, and Mr. Appleyard, sir, was to come here to-morrow forenoon."

"And has Mr. Lavender got no money whatever?" said Sheila's father, with an air that convinced Mrs. Paterson that he was a revengeful man, and was glad that his son-in-law should be so severely punished.

"I don't know, sir," she replied, careful not to go beyond her own sphere.

Sheila came back from the window. She had taken a long time to read and ponder over that letter; though it was not a lengthy one. This was what Frank Lavender had written to his aunt:—

"My dear Aunt Lavender,—I suppose when you read this you will think I am in a bad temper because of what you said to me. It is

not so.   But I am leaving London ; and I wish
to hand over to you before I go the charge of
my house, and to ask you to take possession of
everything in it that does not belong to Sheila.
These things are yours, as you know; and I
have to thank you very much for the loan of
them.   I have to thank you for the far too
liberal allowance you have made me for many
years back.   Will you think I have gone mad
if I ask you to stop that now ?   The fact is, I
am going to have a try at earning something,
for the fun of the thing; and, to make the
experiment satisfactory, I start to-morrow morning for a district in the West Highlands,
where the most ingenious fellow I know couldn't
get a penny-loaf on credit.   You have been
very good to me, Aunt Lavender ; I wish I had
made a better use of your kindness.   So good-
bye just now, and if ever I come back to London
again I shall call on you and thank you in
person.

    " I am, your affectionate nephew,

                    " FRANK LAVENDER."

So far the letter was almost businesslike.
There was no reference to the causes which were
sending him away from London, and which had
already driven him to this extraordinary resolu-

tion about the money he got from his aunt. But at the end of the letter there was a brief postscript, apparently written at the last moment, the words of which were these :—

" Be kind to Sheila. Be as kind to her as I have been cruel to her. In going away from her I feel as though I were exiled by man and forsaken by God."

She came back from the window with the letter in her hand.

"I think you may read it, too, Papa," she said ; for she was anxious that her father should know that Lavender had voluntarily surrendered this money before he was deprived of it. Then she went back to the window.

The slow rain fell from the dismal skies, on the pavement and the railings, and the now almost leafless trees. The atmosphere was filled with a thin white mist, and the people going by were hidden under umbrellas. It was a dreary picture enough ; and yet Sheila was thinking of how much drearier such a day would be on some lonely coast in the north, with the hills obscured behind the rain, and the sea beating hopelessly on the sand. She thought of some small and damp Highland cottage, with narrow windows, a smell of wet wood about, and the

monotonous drip from over the door. And it
seemed to her that a stranger there would be
very lonely, not knowing the ways or the speech
of the simple folk, careless perhaps of his own
comfort, and only listening to the plashing of
the sea and the incessant rain on the bushes and
on the pebbles of the beach. Was there any
picture of desolation, she thought, like that of a
sea under rain, with a slight fog obscuring the
air, and with no wind to stir the pulse with
the noise of waves? And if Frank Lavender
had only gone as far as the Western Highlands,
and was living in some house on the coast, how
sad and still the Atlantic must have been all this
wet forenoon, with the islands of Colonsay and
Oronsay lying remote, and grey, and misty in the
far and desolate plain of the sea.

"It will take a great deal of responsibility
from me, sir," Mrs. Paterson said to old Mackenzie, who was absently thinking of all the
strange possibilities now opening out before him,
"if you will tell me what is to be done. Mrs.
Lavender had no relatives in London, except her
nephew."

"Oh yes," said Mackenzie, waking up; "oh
yes; we will see what is to be done. There will
be the boat wanted for the funeral——"

He recalled himself with an impatient gesture.

"Bless me," he said, "what was I saying? You must ask some one else—you must ask Mr. Ingram. Hef you not sent for Mr. Ingram?"

"Oh yes, sir, I have sent to him; and he will most likely come in the afternoon."

"Then there are the executors mentioned in the will—that wass something you should know about; and they will tell you what to do. As for me, it is ferry little I will know about such things."

"Perhaps your daughter, sir," suggested Mrs. Paterson, "would tell me what she thinks should be done with the rooms——And as for luncheon, sir, if you would wait——"

"Oh, my daughter?" said Mr. Mackenzie, as if struck by a new idea, but determined all the same that Sheila should not have this new responsibility thrust on her. "My daughter?— well, you wass saying, mem, that my daughter would help you? Oh yes, but she is a ferry young thing, and you wass saying we must hef luncheon? Oh yes, but we will not give you so much trouble, and we hef luncheon ordered at the other house whatever; and there is the young girl there that we cannot leave all by herself. And you hef a great experience, mem, and whatever you do, that will be right; do not have any fear of that. And I will come round when

you want me—oh yes, I will come round at any
time; but my daughter, she is a ferry young
thing, and she would be of no use to you whatever—none whatever. And when Mr. Ingram
comes you will send him round to the place where
my daughter is, for we will want to see him, if
he hass the time to come. But where is
Sheila ? "

Sheila had quietly left the room and stolen
into the silent chamber in which the dead woman
lay. They found her standing close by the
bedside, almost in a trance.

" Sheila," said her father, taking her hand,
" come away now, like a good girl. It is no
use your waiting here ; and Mairi—what will
Mairi be doing ? "

She suffered herself to be led away; and
they went home and had luncheon, but the girl
could not eat for the notion that somewhere or
other a pair of eyes were looking at her, and
were hideously laughing at her, as if to remind
her of the prophecy of that old woman, that
her friends would sit down to a comfortable
meal and begin to wonder what sort of mourning
they would have.

It was not until the evening that Ingram
called. He had been greatly surprised to hear
from Mrs. Paterson that Mr. Mackenzie had been

there, along with his daughter; and he now expected to find the old King of Borva in a towering passion. He found him, on the contrary, as bland and as pleased as decency would admit of in view of the tragedy that had occurred in the morning; and, indeed, as Mackenzie had never seen Mrs. Lavender, there was less reason why he should wear the outward semblance of grief. Sheila's father asked her to go out of the room for a little while; and when she and Mairi had gone, he said cheerfully—

"Well, Mr. Ingram, and it is a rich man you are at last."

"Mrs. Paterson said she had told you," Ingram said, with a shrug. "You never expected to find me rich, did you?"

"Never," said Mackenzie, frankly. "But it is a ferry good thing—oh yes, it is a ferry good thing—to hef money and be independent of people. And you will make a good use of it, I know."

"You don't seem disposed, sir, to regret that Lavender has been robbed of what should have belonged to him?"

"Oh, not at all," said Mackenzie, gravely and cautiously, for he did not want his plans to be displayed prematurely. "But I hef no quarrel with him; so you will not think I am glad to hef the money taken away for that. Oh no; I hef seen a great many men and women; and it wass no strange thing that these two young ones living all by themselves in London, should hef a quarrel. But it will come all right again if we do not make too much about it. If they like one another, they will soon come together again, tek my word for it, Mr. Ingram; and I hef seen a great many men and women. And as for the money—well, as for the money, I hef plenty for my Sheila, and she will not starve when I die, no, nor before that either; and as for the poor old woman that has died, I am ferry glad she left her money to one that will make a good use of it, and will not throw it away whatever."

"Oh, but you know, Mr. Mackenzie, you are congratulating me without cause. I must tell you how the matter stands. The money does not belong to me at all—Mrs. Lavender never intended it should. It was meant to go to Sheila——"

"Oh, I know, I know," said Mr. Mackenzie, with a wave of his hand. "I wass hearing all that from the woman at the house. But how will you know what Mrs. Lavender intended? You hef only that woman's story of it. And here is the will, and you hef the money, and—and——"

Mackenzie hesitated for a moment; and then said with a sudden vehemence—

"——and, by Kott, you shall keep it!"

Ingram was a trifle startled.

"But look here, sir," he said, in a tone of expostulation, "you make a mistake. I myself know Mrs. Lavender's intentions. I don't go by any story of Mrs. Paterson's. Mrs. Lavender made over the money to me with express injunctions to place it at the disposal of Sheila whenever I should see fit. Oh, there's no mistake about it, so you need not protest, sir. If the money belonged to me, I should be delighted to keep it. No man in the country more desires to be rich than I; so don't fancy I am flinging away a fortune out of generosity. If any rich and kind-hearted old lady will send me £5,000 or £10,000, you will see how I shall stick to it. But the simple truth is, this money is not mine at all. It was never intended to be mine. It belongs to Sheila."

Ingram talked in a very matter-of-fact way; the old man feared what he said was true.

"Ay, it is a ferry good story," said Mackenzie, cautiously, "and may be it is all true. And you wass saying you would like to hef money?"

"I most decidedly should like to have money."

"Well, then," said the old man, watching his

friend's face, "there iss no one to say that the story is true; and who will believe it? And if Sheila wass to come to you and say she did not believe it, and she would not hef the money from you, you would hef to keep it, eh?"

Ingram's sallow face blushed crimson.

"I don't know what you mean," he said, stiffly. "Do you propose to pervert the girl's mind, and make me a party to a fraud?"

"Oh, there is no use getting into an anger," said Mackenzie, suavely, "when common sense will do as well whatever. And there wass no perversion, and there wass no fraud talked about. It wass just this, Mr. Ingram, that if the old lady's will leaves you her property, who will you be getting to believe that she did not mean to give it to you?"

"I tell you now whom she meant to give it to," said Ingram, still somewhat hotly.

"Oh yes, oh yes, that is ferry well But who will believe it?"

"Good heavens, sir, who will believe I could be such a fool as to fling away this property if it belonged to me?"

"They will think you a fool to do it now— yes, that is sure enough," said Mackenzie.

"I don't care what they think. And it seems rather odd, Mr. Mackenzie, that you should be trying to deprive your own daughter of what belongs to her."

"Oh, my daughter is ferry well off whatever —she does not want anyone's money," said Mackenzie; and then a new notion struck him. "Will you tell me this, Mr. Ingram? If Mrs. Lavender left you her property in this way, what for did she want to change her will, eh?"

"Well, to tell you the truth, I refused to take the responsibility. She was anxious to have this money given to Sheila so that Lavender should not touch it—and I don't think it was a wise intention, for there is not a prouder man in the world than Lavender, and I know that Sheila would not consent to hold a penny that did not equally belong to him. However, that was her notion; and I was the first victim of it. I protested against it; and I suppose that set her to inquiring whether the money could not be absolutely bequeathed to Sheila direct. I don't know anything about it myself; but that's how the matter stands as far as I'm concerned."

"But you will think it over, Mr. Ingram," said Mackenzie quietly; "you will think it over and be in no hurry. It is not every man that hass a lot of money given to him. And it is no wrong to my Sheila at all: for she will hef quite plenty; and she would be ferry sorry to take the money away from you, that is sure enough; and you will not be hasty, Mr. Ingram, but be cautious and reasonable, and you will see the money will do you far more good than it would do to my Sheila."

Ingram began to think that he had tied a millstone round his neck.

CHAPTER V.

IN EXILE.

ONE evening, in the olden time, Lavender and Sheila and Ingram and old Mackenzie were all sitting high up on the rocks near Borvabost, chatting to each other, and watching the red light pale on the bosom of the Atlantic as the sun sank behind the edge of the world. Ingram was smoking a wooden pipe. Lavender sat with Sheila's hand in his. The old King of Borva was discoursing of the fishing populations round the western coasts, and of their various ways and habits.

"I wish I could have seen Tarbert," Lavender was saying, "but the *Iona* just passes the mouth of the little harbour as she comes up Loch Fyne. I know two or three men who go there every year to paint the fishing life of the place. It is an odd little place, isn't it?"

"Tarbert?" said Mr. Mackenzie; "you wass

wanting to know about Tarbert? Ah, well, it is getting to be a better place now, but a year or two ago it wass ferry like hell. Oh, yes, it wass, Sheila, so you need not say anything. And this wass the way of it, Mr. Lavender, that the trawling was not made legal then, and the men they were just like teffles, with the swearing, and the drinking, and the fighting that went on; and if you went into the harbour in the open day, you would find them drunk, and fighting, and some of them with blood on their faces, for it wass a ferry wild time. It wass many a one will say that the Tarbert men would run down the police-boat some dark night. And what wass the use of catching the trawlers now and again, and taking their boats and their nets to be sold at Greenock, when they would go themselves over to Greenock, to the auction, and buy them back? Oh, it wass a great deal of money they made then— I hef heard of a crew of eight men getting £30 each man in the course of one night, and that not seldom mirover."

"But why didn't the Government put it down?" Lavender asked.

"Well, you see," Mackenzie answered, with the air of a man well acquainted with the diffi- culties of ruling; "you see that it wass not quite sure that the trawling did much harm to the fishing. And the *Jackal*—that wass the Government steamer—she wass not much good in getting the better of the Tarbert men, who are ferry good with their boats in the rowing, and are ferry cunning whatever. For the buying boats they would go out to sea, and take the herring there, and then the trawlers they would sink their nets and come home in the morning as if they had not caught one fish, although the boat would be white with the scales of the herring. And what is more, sir, the Government knew ferry well that if trawling wass put down then, there would be a ferry good many murders; for the Tarbert men, when they came home to driuk whisky, and wash the whisky down with porter, they were ready to fight anybody."

"It must be a delightful place to live in," Lavender said.

"Oh, but it is ferry different now," Mackenzie continued, "ferry different. The men they are nearly all Good Templars now, and there is no drinking whatever, and there is reading-rooms and such things, and the place is ferry quiet and respectable."

"I hear," Ingram remarked, "that good people attribute the change to moral suasion, and that wicked people put it down to want of money."

"Papa, this boy will have to be put to bed," Sheila said.

"Well," Mackenzie answered, "there is not so much money in the place as there wass in the old times. The shopkeepers do not make so much money as before, when the men were wild and drunk in the day-time, and had plenty to spend when the police-boat did not catch them. But the fishermen they are ferry much better without the money; and I can say for them, Mr. Lavender, that there is no better fishermen on the coast. They are ferry fine, tall men; and they are ferry well dressed in their blue clothes; and they are manly fellows, whether they are drunk or whether they are sober. Now look at this, sir, that in the worst of weather they will neffer tek whisky with them when they go out to the sea at night, for they think it is cowardly. And they are ferry fine fellows and gentlemanly in their ways, and they are ferry good-natured to strangers."

"I have heard that of them on all hands," Lavender said, "and some day I hope to put their civility and good fellowship to the proof."

That was merely the idle conversation of a summer evening; no one paid any further attention to it, nor did even Lavender himself think again of his vaguely-expressed hope of some day visiting Tarbert. Let us now shift the scene of this narrative to Tarbert itself.

When you pass from the broad and blue waters of Loch Fyne into the narrow and rocky channel leading to Tarbert harbour, you find before you an almost circular bay, round which stretches an irregular line of white houses. There is an abundance of fishing-craft in the harbour, lying in careless and picturesque groups, with their brown hulls and spars sending a ruddy reflection down on the lapping water, which is green under the shadow of each boat. Along the shore stand the tall poles on which the fishermen dry their nets; and above these, on the summit of a rocky crag, rise the ruins of an old castle, with the daylight shining through the empty windows. Beyond the houses, again, lie successive lines of hills, at this moment lit up by shafts of sunlight that lend a glowing warmth and richness to the fine colours of a late autumn. The hills are red and brown with rusted bracken and heather; and here and there the smooth waters of the bay catch a tinge of their varied hues. In one of the fishing-smacks that lie almost underneath the shadow of the tall crag on which the castle ruins stand, an artist has put up a rough-and-ready easel, and is apparently busy at work painting a group of boats just beyond. Some indication of the rich colours of the craft—their ruddy sails, brown nets and bladders, and their varnished but not painted hulls—already appears on the canvas; and by and by some vision may arise of the far hills in their soft autumnal tints and of the bold blue and white sky moving overhead. Perhaps the old man who is smoking in the stern of one of the boats has been placed there on purpose. A boy seated on some nets occasionally casts an anxious glance towards the painter, as if to inquire when his penance will be over.

A small open boat, with a heap of stones for ballast, and with no great elegance in shape of rigging, comes slowly in from the mouth of the harbour, and is gently run alongside the boat in which the man is painting. A fresh-coloured young fellow, with plenty of curly brown hair, who has dressed himself as a yachtsman, calls out—

"Lavender, do you know the *White Rose*, a big schooner yacht, about eighty tons I should think?"

"Yes," Lavender said, without turning round or taking his eyes off the canvas.

"Whose is she?"

" Lord Newstead's."

" Well, either he or his skipper hailed me just now and wanted to know whether you were here. I said you were. The fellow asked me if I was going into the harbour. I said I was. So he gave me a message for you; that they would hang about outside for half an hour or so, if you would go out to them, and take a run up to Ardishaig."

" I can't, Johnny."

" I'd take you out, you know."

" I don't want to go."

" But look here, Lavender," said the younger man, seizing hold of Lavender's boat, and causing the easel to shake dangerously; " he asked me to luncheon, too."

" Why don't you go, then?" was the only reply, uttered rather absently.

" I can't go without you."

" Well, I don't mean to go."

The younger man looked vexed for a moment, and then said, in a tone of expostulation—

" You know it is very absurd of you going on like this, Lavender. No fellow can paint decently if he gets out of bed in the middle of the night and waits for daylight to rush up to his easel. How many hours have you been at work already to-day? If you don't give your eyes a

rest, they will get colour-blind to a dead certainty. Do you think you will paint the whole
place off the face of the earth, now that the
other fellows have gone?"

"I can't be bothered talking to you, Johnny.
You'll make me throw something at you. Go
away."

"I think it's rather mean, you know," continued the persistent Johnny, "for a fellow like
you, who doesn't need it, to come and fill the
market all at once, while we unfortunate devils
can scarcely get a crust. And there are two
heron just round the point, and I have my
breechloader and a dozen cartridges here."

"Go away, Johnny,"—that was all the answer
he got.

"I'll go out and tell Lord Newstead that you
are a cantankerous brute. I suppose he'll have
the decency to offer me luncheon; and I dare
say I could get him a shot at these heron. You
are a fool not to come, Lavender;" and, so
saying, the young man put out again, and he
was heard to go away talking to himself about
obstinate idiots, and greed, and the certainty of
getting a shot at the heron.

When he had quite gone, Lavender, who had
scarcely raised his eyes from his work, suddenly
put down his palette and brushes—he almost

dropped them, indeed—and quickly put up both his hands to his head, pressing them on the side of his temples. The old fisherman in the boat beyond noticed this strange movement, and forthwith caught a rope, hauled the boat across a stretch of water, and then came scrambling over bowsprits, lowered sails, and nets, to where Lavender had just sat down.

"Wass there anything the matter, sir?" he said, with much evidence of concern.

"My head is a little bad, Donald," Lavender said, still pressing his hands on his temple, as if to get rid of some strange feeling; "I wish you would pull in to the shore and get me some whisky."

"Oh ay," said the old man, hastily scrambling into the little black boat lying beside the smack; "and it is no wonder to me this will come to you, sir, for I hef never seen any of the gentlemen so long at the pentin as you—from the morning till the night—and it is no wonder to me this will come to you. But I will get you the whushkey—it is a grand thing, the whushkey."

The old fisherman was not long in getting ashore, and running up to the cottage in which Lavender lived, and getting a bottle of whisky and a glass. Then he got down to the boat again, and was surprised that he could nowhere see Mr. Lavender on board the smack. Perhaps he had lain down on the nets in the bottom of the boat.

When Donald got out to the smack, he found the young man lying insensible, his face white, and his teeth clenched. With something of a cry, the old fisherman jumped into the boat, knelt down, and proceeded in a rough and ready fashion to force some whisky into Lavender's mouth.

"Oh ay, oh yes, it is a grand thing, the whushkey," he muttered to himself; "oh yes, sir, you must hef some more—it is no matter if you will choke—it is ferry goot whushkey, and will do you no harm whatever—and, oh yes, sir, that is ferry well, and you are all right again, and you will sit quite quiet now, and you will hef a little more whushkey."

The young man looked round him.

"Have you been ashore, Donald? Oh, yes; I suppose so. Did I fall down? Well, I am all right now; it was the glare of the sea that made me giddy. Take a dram for yourself, Donald."

"There is but one glass, sir," said Donald, who had picked up something of the notions of gentlefolks, "but I will just tek the bottle;"

and so, to avoid drinking out of the same glass (which was rather a small one), he was good enough to take a pull, and a strong pull, at the black bottle. Then he heaved a sigh, and wiped the top of the bottle with his sleeve.

" Yes, as I was saying, sir, there was none of the gentlemen I hef effer seen in Tarbert will keep at the penten so long ass you; and many of them will be stronger ass you and will be more accustomed to it whatever. But when a man iss making money—" and Donald shook his head; he knew it was useless to argue.

" But I am not making money, Donald," Lavender said, still looking a trifle pale. " I doubt whether I have made as much as you have since I came to Tarbert."

" Oh yes," said Donald, contentedly, " all the gentlemen will say that. They never hef any money. But wass you ever with them when they could not get a dram because they had no money to pay for it ? "

Donald's test of impecuniosity could not be gainsayed. Lavender laughed, and bade him get back into the other boat.

" Deed I will not," said Donald, sturdily.

Lavender stared at him.

" Oh no; you wass doing quite enough the day already, or you would not hef tumbled into the boat whatever. And supposing that you wass to hef tumbled into the water, you would have been trooned as sure as you wass alive."

"And a good job too, Donald," said the younger man, idly looking at the lapping green water.

Donald shook his head gravely.

"You would not say that if you had friends of yours that wass trooned, and if you had seen them when they went down in the water."

"They say it is an easy death, Donald."

"They neffer tried it that said that," said the old fisherman, gloomily. "It wass one day the son of my sister wass coming over from Saltcoats —but I hef no wish to speak of it; and that wass but one among ferry many that I have known."

"How long is it since you were in the Lewis, did you say?" Lavender asked, changing the subject. Donald was accustomed to have the talk suddenly diverted into this channel. He could not tell why the young English stranger wanted him continually to be talking about the Lewis.

"Oh, it is many and many a year ago, as I hef said; and you will know far more about the Lewis than I will. But Stornoway, that is a fine big town; and I hef a cousin there that keeps a shop, and is a ferry rich man whatever, and many's the time he will ask me to come and see him. And if the Lord be spared, maybe I will some day."

" You mean if you be spared, Donald."

" Oh aye ; it is all wan," said Donald.

Lavender had brought with him some bread and cheese in a piece of paper, for luncheon ; and this store of frugal provisions having been opened out, the old fisherman was invited to join in ; an invitation he gravely, but not eagerly, accepted. He took off his blue bonnet and said grace ; then he took the bread and cheese in his hand, and looked round inquiringly. There was a stone jar of water in the bottom of the boat ; that was not what Donald was looking after. Lavender handed him the black bottle he had brought out from the cottage, which was more to his mind. And then, this humble meal despatched, the old man was persuaded to go back to his post, and Lavender continued his work.

The short afternoon was drawing to a close when young Johnny Eyre came sailing in from Loch Fyne, himself and a boy of ten or twelve managing that crank little boat with its top-heavy sails.

" Are you at work yet, Lavender ? " he said. " I never saw such a beggar. It's getting quite dark."

"What sort of luncheon did Newstead give you, Johnny?"

"Oh, something worth going for, I can tell you. You want to live in Tarbert for a month or two to find out the value of decent cooking and good wine. He was awfully surprised when I described this place to him. He wouldn't believe you were living here in a cottage—I said a garret, for I pitched it hot and strong, mind you. I said you were living in a garret, that you never saw a razor, and lived on oatmeal porridge and whisky, and that your only amusement was going out at night and risking your neck in this delightful boat of mine. You should have seen him examining this remarkable vessel. And there were two ladies on board, and they were asking after you, too."

"Who were they?"

"I don't know. I didn't catch their names when I was introduced; but the noble skipper called one of them Polly."

"Oh, I know."

"Ain't you coming ashore, Lavender? You can't see to work now."

"All right. I shall put my traps ashore; and then I'll have a run with you down Loch Fyne, if you like, Johnny."

"Well, I don't like," said the handsome lad,

frankly ; " for it's looking rather squally about. It seems to me you're bent on drowning yourself. Before those other fellows went, they came to the conclusion that you had committed a murder."

" Did they really ? " Lavender said, with little interest.

" And if you go away and live in that wild place you were talking of during the winter, they will be quite sure of it. Why, man, you'd come back with your hair turned white. You might as well think of living by yourself at the Arctic Pole."

Neither Johnny Eyre nor any of the men who had just left Tarbert knew anything of Frank Lavender's recent history ; and Lavender himself was not disposed to be communicative. They would know soon enough when they went up to London. In the meantime they were surprised to find that Lavender's habits were very singularly altered. He had grown miserly. They laughed when he told them he had no money ; and he did not seek to persuade them of the fact ; but it was clear, at all events, that none of them lived so frugally, or worked so anxiously, as he. Then, when his work was done in the evening, and when they met alter- nately at each other's rooms, to dine off mutton and potatoes, with a glass of whisky, and a pipe, and a game of cards to follow, what was the meaning of those sudden fits of silence that would strike in when the general hilarity was at its pitch? And what was the meaning of the utter recklessness he displayed when they would go out of an evening in their open sailing-boats to shoot sea-fowl, or make a voyage along the rocky coast in the dead of night, to wait for the dawn to show them the haunts of the seals? The Lavender they had met occasionally in London was a fastidious, dilettante, self-possessed, and yet not disagreeable young fellow; this man was almost pathetically anxious about his work, oftentimes he was morose and silent, and then again there was no sort of danger or difficulty he was not ready to plunge into when they were sailing about that iron-bound coast. They could not make it out; but the joke among themselves was that he had committed a murder, and therefore had grown reckless.

This Johnny Eyre was not much of an artist; but he liked the society of artists; he had a little money of his own, plenty of time, and a love of boating and shooting; and so he had pitched his tent at Tarbert, and was proud to cherish the delusion that he was working hard and earning fame and wealth. As a matter of fact, he never earned anything; but he had very good spirits, and living in Tarbert is cheap.

From the moment that Lavender had come to the place, Johnny Eyre made him his special companion. He had a great respect for a man who could shoot anything anywhere; and when he and Lavender came back together from a cruise, there was no use saying which had actually done the brilliant deeds the evidence of which was carried ashore. But Lavender, oddly enough, knew little about sailing; and Johnny was pleased to assume the airs of an instructor on this point; his only difficulty being that his pupil had more than the ordinary hardihood of an ignoramus, and was inclined to do reckless things even after he had sufficient skill to know that they were dangerous.

Lavender got into the small boat, taking his canvas with him, but leaving his easel in the fishing-smack. He pulled himself and Johnny Eyre ashore; they scrambled up the rocks and into the road; and then they went into the small white cottage in which Lavender lived. The picture was, for greater safety, left in Lavender's bedroom, which already contained about a dozen canvases with sketches in various stages on them. Then he went out to his friend again.

"I've had a long day to-day, Johnny. I wish you'd go out with me; the excitement of a squall would clear one's brain, I fancy."

"Oh, I'll go out if you like," Eyre said; "but I shall take very good care to run in before the squall comes, if there's any about. I don't think there will be, after all. I fancied I saw a flash of lightning about half an hour ago, down in the south; but nothing has come of it. There are some curlew about; and the guillemots are in thousands. You don't seem to care about shooting guillemots, Lavender."

"Well, you see, potting a bird that is sitting on the water ——" said Lavender with a shrug.

"Oh, it isn't as easy as you might imagine. Of course, you could kill them if you liked, but everybody ain't such a swell as you are with a gun; and, mind you, it's uncommonly awkward to catch the right moment for firing when the bird goes bobbing up and down on the waves, disappearing altogether every second. I think it's very good fun myself. It is very exciting when you don't know the moment the bird will dive, and whether you can afford to go any nearer. And as for shooting them on the water, you have to do that; for when do you get a chance of shooting them flying?"

"I don't see much necessity for shooting them at any time," said Lavender, as he went down to the shore again, "but I am glad to see you get some amusement out of it. Have you got cartridges with you? Is your gun in the boat?."

"Yes. Come along. We'll have a run out, anyhow."

When they pulled out again to that cockle-shell craft with its stone ballast and big brown mainsail, the boy was sent ashore, and the two companions set out by themselves. By this time the sun had gone down, and a strange green twilight was shining over the sea. As they got further out, the dusky shores seemed to have a pale mist hanging around them; but there were no clouds on the hills, for a clear sky shone overhead, awaiting the coming of the stars. Strange, indeed, was the silence out here, broken only by the lapping of the water on the sides of the boat, and the calling of birds in the distance. Far away the orange ray of a lighthouse began to quiver in the lambent dusk. The pale green light on the waves did not die out; but the shadows grew darker, so that Eyre, with his gun close at hand, could not make out his groups of guillemots, although he heard them calling all around. They had come out too late, indeed, for any such purpose.

Thither, on those beautiful evenings, after his day's work was over, Lavender was accustomed to come, either by himself or with his present companion. Johnny Eyre did not intrude on his solitude ; he was invariably too eager to get a shot, his chief delight being to get to the bow, to let the boat drift for a while silently through the waves, so that she might come unawares on some flock of sea-birds. Lavender, sitting in the stern, with the tiller in his hand, was really alone in this world of water and sky, with all the majesty of the night and the stars around him.

And on these occasions he used to sit and dream of the beautiful time long ago in Loch Roag, when nights such as these used to come over the Atlantic, and find Sheila and himself sailing on the peaceful waters, or seated high up on the rocks listening to the murmur of the tide. Here was the same strange silence, the same solemn and pale light in the sky, the same mystery of the moving plain all around them that seemed somehow to be alive and yet voiceless and sad. Many a time his heart became so full of recollections, that he had almost called aloud "Sheila ! Sheila ! " and waited for the sea and the sky to answer him with the sound of her voice. In these bygone days he had pleased himself with the fancy that the girl was somehow the product of all the beautiful aspects of nature around her. It was the sea that was in her eyes ; it was the fair sunlight that shone in her face ; the breath of her life was the breath of the moorland winds. He had written verses about this fancy of hers ; and he had conveyed them secretly to her, sure that she, at least, would find no defects in them. And many a time, far away from Loch Roag, and from Sheila, lines of this conceit would wander through his brain, set to the saddest of all music, the music of irreparable loss. What did they say to him now that he recalled them like some half-forgotten voice out of the strange past ?—

For she, and the clouds, and the breezes were one,
And the hills and the sea had conspired with the sun
To charm and bewilder all men with the grace
They combined and conferred on her wonderful face.

   *   *   *   *   *

The sea lapped around the boat ; the green light on the waves grew less intense ; in the silence the first of the stars came out ; and somehow the time in which he had seen Sheila in these rare and magical colours seemed to become more and more remote.

   *   *   *   *   *

An angel in passing looked downward and smiled,
And carried to heaven the fame of the child ;
And then what the waves and the sky and the sun
And the tremulous breath of the hills had begun,
Required but one touch. To finish the whole,
God loved her, and gave her a beautiful soul !

And what had he done with this rare treasure entrusted to him? His companions, jesting among themselves, had said that he had committed a murder; in his own heart there was something at this moment of a murderer's remorse.

Johnny Eyre uttered a short cry. Lavender looked ahead, and saw that some black object was disappearing among the waves.

"What a fright I got!" Eyre said, with a laugh. "I never saw the fellow come near; and he came up just below the bowsprit. He came heeling over as quiet as a mouse. I say, Lavender, I think we might as well cut it now; my eyes are quite bewildered with the light on the water; I couldn't make out a kraken if it was coming across our bows."

"Don't be in a hurry, Johnny. We'll put her out a bit, and then let her drift back. I want to tell you a story."

"Oh, all right," he said; and so they put her head round, and soon she was lying over before the breeze, and slowly drawing away from those outlines of the coast which showed them where Tarbert harbour cut into the land. And then, once more, they let her drift, and young Eyre took a nip of whisky and settled himself so as to hear Lavender's story, whatever it might be.

" You knew I was married ? "

" Yes."

" Didn't you ever wonder why my wife did not come here ? "

" Why should I wonder ? Plenty of fellows have to spend half the year apart from their wives ; the only thing in your case I couldn't understand was the necessity for your doing it. For you know that's all nonsense about your want of funds."

" It isn't nonsense, Johnny. But now, if you like, I will tell you why my wife has never come here."

Then he told the story, out there under the stars, with no thought of interruption, for there was a world of moving water around them. It was the first time he had let anyone into his confidence ; and perhaps the darkness aided his revelations ; but at any rate he went over all the old time until it seemed to his companion that he was talking to himself, so aimless and desultory were his pathetic reminiscences. He called her Sheila, though Eyre had never heard her name. He spoke of her father as though Eyre must have known him. And yet this rambling series of confession, and self-reproaches, and tender memories, did form a certain sort of narrative, so that the young fellow sitting quietly in the boat there got a pretty fair notion of what had happened.

"You are an unlucky fellow," he said to Lavender. "I never heard anything like that. But you know you must have exaggerated a good deal about it—I should like to hear her story. I am sure you could not have treated her like that."

"God knows how I did, but the truth is just as I have told you; and although I was blind enough at the time, I can read the whole story now in letters of fire. I hope you will never have such a thing constantly before your eyes, Johnny."

The lad was silent for some time; and then he said rather timidly—

"Do you think, Lavender, she knows how sorry you are?"

"If she did, what good would that do?" said the other.

"Women are awfully forgiving, you know," Johnny said, in a hesitating fashion. "I--I don't think it is quite fair not to give her a chance—a chance of—of being generous, you know. You know, I think the better a woman is, the more inclined she is to be charitable to other folks who mayn't be quite up to the mark, you know; and you see, it ain't everyone who can claim to be always doing the right thing; and the next best thing to that is to be sorry for what you've done and try to do better. It's rather cheeky, you know, my advising you—or trying to make you pluck up your spirits—but I'll tell you what it is, Lavender, if I knew her well enough I'd go straight to her to-morrow, and I'd put in a good word for you, and tell her some things she doesn't know, and you'd see if she wouldn't write you a letter, or even come and see you——"

" That is all nonsense, Johnny, though it's very good of you to think of it. The mischief I have done isn't to be put aside by the mere writing of a letter——"

" But it seems to me," Johnny said, with some warmth, " that you are as unfair to her as to yourself in not giving her a chance. You don't know how willing she may be to overlook everything that is past——"

" If she were, I am not fit to go near her. I couldn't have the cheek to try, Johnny."

" But what more can you be than sorry for what is past?" said the younger fellow, persistently. " And you don't know how pleased it makes a good woman to give her a chance of forgiving anybody. And if we were all to set up for being archangels, and if there was to be

M 2

no sort of getting back for us after we had made a slip, where should we be? And in place of going to her, and making it all right, you start away for the Sound of Islay, and, by Jove, won't you find out what spending a winter under these Jura mountains means!"

A flash of lightning — somewhere down among the Arran hills—interrupted the speaker, and drew the attention of the two young men to the fact that in the east and south-east the stars were no longer visible, while something of a brisk breeze had sprung up.

"This breeze will take us back splendidly," Johnny said, getting ready again for the run in to Tarbert.

He had scarcely spoken when Lavender called attention to a fishing-smack that was apparently making for the harbour. With all sails set, she was sweeping by them like some black phantom across the dark plain of the sea. They could not make out the figures on board of her; but as she passed, some one called out to them.

"What did he say?" Lavender asked.

"I don't know," his companion said, "but it was some sort of warning, I suppose. By Jove, Lavender, what is that?"

Behind them there was a strange hissing and

rumbling noise that the wind brought along to
them, but nothing could be seen.

" Rain, isn't it ? " Lavender said.

" There never was rain like that," his companion said. " That is a squall, and it will be
here presently. We must haul down the sails—
for God's sake, look sharp, Lavender ! "

There was certainly no time to lose, for the
noise behind them was increasing and deepening
into a roar ; and the heavens had grown black
overhead, so that the spars and ropes of the
crank little boat could scarcely be made out.
They had just got the sails down when the first
gust of the squall struck the boat as with a
blow of iron, and sent her staggering forward
into the trough of the sea. Then all around
them came the fury of the storm ; and the cause
of the sound they had heard was apparent in
the foaming water that was torn and scattered
abroad by the gale. Up from the black south-
east came the fierce hurricane, sweeping everything before it, and hurling this creaking and
straining boat about as if it were a cork. They
could see little of the sea around them, but they
could hear the awful noise of it, and they knew
they were being swept along on those hurrying
waves, towards a coast which was invisible in
the blackness of the night.

"Johnny, we'll never make the harbour. I can't see a light," Lavender cried. "Hadn't we better try to keep her up the loch?"

"We *must* make the harbour," his companion said; "she can't stand this much longer."

Blinding torrents of rain were now being driven down by the force of the wind, so that all around them nothing was visible but a wild boiling and seething of clouds and waves. Eyre was up at the bow, trying to catch some glimpse of the outlines of the coast, or to make out some light that would show them where the entrance to Tarbert harbour lay. If only some lurid shaft of lightning would pierce the gloom!—for they knew that they were being driven headlong on an iron-bound coast, and amid all the noise of the wind and the sea they listened with a fear that had no words for the first roar of the waves along the rocks.

Suddenly Lavender heard a shrill scream— almost like the cry that a hare gives when it finds the dog's fangs in its neck; and at the same moment, amid all the darkness of the night, a still blacker object seemed to start out of the gloom, right ahead of them. The boy had no time to shout any warning beyond that cry of despair; for with a wild crash the boat struck on the rocks, rose and struck again, and was then dashed over by a heavy sea, both of its occupants being thrown into the fierce swirls of foam that were dashing in and through the rocky channels. Strangely enough they were thrown together; and Lavender, clinging to the seaweed, instinctively laid hold of his companion just as the latter appeared to be slipping into the gulf beneath.

"Johnny," he cried, "hold on! hold on to me, or we shall both go in a minute."

But the lad had no life left in him, and lay like a log there, while each wave that struck and rolled hissing and gurgling through the channels between the rocks, seemed to drag at him and seek to suck him down into the darkness. With one despairing effort Lavender struggled to get him further up on the slippery seaweed, and succeeded. But his success had lost him his own vantage-ground; and he knew that he was going down into the swirling waters beneath, close by the broken boat that was still being dashed about by the waves.

CHAPTER VI.

"HAME FAIN WOULD I BE."

UNEXPECTED circumstances had detained Mrs. Kavanagh and her daughter in London long after everybody else had left; but at length they were ready to start for their projected trip into Switzerland. On the day before their departure Ingram dined with them—on his own invitation. He had got into a habit of letting them know when it would suit him to devote an evening to their instruction; and it was difficult, indeed, to say which of the two ladies submitted the more readily and meekly to the dictatorial enunciation of his opinions. Mrs. Kavanagh, it is true, sometimes dissented in so far as a smile indicated dissent; but her daughter scarcely reserved to herself so much liberty. Mr. Ingram had taken her in hand; and expected of her the obedience and respect due to his superior age.

And yet, somehow or other, he occasionally

found himself indirectly soliciting the advice of this gentle, clear-eyed, and clear-headed young person, more especially as regarded the difficulties surrounding Sheila; and sometimes a chance remark of hers, uttered in a timid, or careless, or even mocking fashion, would astonish him by the rapid light it threw on these dark troubles. On this evening—the last evening they were spending in London—it was his own affairs which he proposed to mention to Mrs. Lorraine; and he had no more hesitation in doing so than if she had been his oldest friend. He wanted to ask her what he should do about the money that Mrs. Lavender had left him; and he intended to be a good deal more frank with Mrs. Lorraine than with any of the others to whom he had spoken about the matter. For he was well aware that Mrs. Lavender had at first resolved that he should have at least a considerable portion of her wealth; or why should she have asked him how he would like to be a rich man?

"I do not think," said Mrs. Lorraine, quietly, "that there is much use in your asking me what you should do; for I know what you will do, whether it accords with anyone's opinion or no. And yet you would find a great advantage in having money."

"Oh, I know that," he said readily. "I should like to be rich beyond anything that ever happened in a drama; and I should take my chance of all the evil influences that money is supposed to exert. Do you know, I think you rich people are very unfairly treated—"

"But we are not rich," said Mrs. Kavanagh, passing at the time. "Cecilia and I find ourselves very poor sometimes."

"But I quite agree with Mr. Ingram, Mamma," said Cecilia, as if anyone had the courage to disagree with Mr. Ingram; "rich people are shamefully ill-treated. If you go to a theatre, now, you find that all the virtues are on the side of the poor; and if there are a few vices, you get a thousand excuses for them. No one takes account of the temptations of the rich. You have people educated from their infancy to imagine that the whole world was made for them—every wish they have, gratified —every day showing them people dependent on them and grateful for favours; and no allowance is made for such a temptation to become haughty, self-willed, and overbearing. But of course it stands to reason that the rich never have justice done them in plays and stories; for the people who write are poor."

"Not all of them."

" But enough to strike an average of injustice. And it is very hard. For it is the rich who buy books and who take boxes at the theatres, and then they find themselves grossly abused; whereas the humble peasant who can scarcely read at all, and who never pays more than sixpence for a seat in the gallery, is flattered, and coaxed, and caressed until one wonders whether the source of virtue is the drinking of sour ale. Mr. Ingram, you do it yourself. You impress Mamma and me with the belief that we are miserable sinners if we are not continually doing some act of charity. Well, that is all very pleasant and necessary, in moderation; but you don't find the poor folks so very anxious to live for other people. They don't care much what becomes of us. They take your port wine and flannels as if they were conferring a favour on you; but as for *your* condition and prospects, in this world and the next, they don't trouble much about that. Now, Mamma, just wait a moment——"

" I will not. You are a bad girl," said Mrs. Kavanagh, severely. "Here has Mr. Ingram been teaching you and making you better for ever so long back, and you pretend to accept his counsel and reform yourself; and then all at once you break out, and throw down the tablets of the law, and conduct yourself like a heathen."

"Because I want him to explain, Mamma. I suppose he considers it wicked of us to start for Switzerland to-morrow. The money we shall spend in travelling might have despatched a cargo of muskets to some missionary station, so that——"

"Cecilia!"

"Oh no," Ingram said, carelessly, and nursing his knee with both his hands as usual, "travelling is not wicked—it is only unreasonable. A traveller, you know, is a person who has a house in one town, and who goes to live in a house in another town, in order to have the pleasure of paying for both."

"Mr. Ingram," said Mrs. Kavanagh, "will you talk seriously for one minute, and tell me whether we are to expect to see you in the Tyrol?"

But Ingram was not in a mood for talking seriously; and he waited to hear Mrs. Lorraine strike in with some calmly audacious invitation. She did not, however; and he turned round from her mother to question her. He was surprised to find that her eyes were fixed on the ground, and that something like a tinge of colour was in her face. He turned rapidly away again.

" Well, Mrs. Kavanagh," he said, with a fine
air of indifference, "the last time we spoke
about that, I was not in the difficulty I am in
at present. How could I go travelling just
now, without knowing how to regulate my
daily expenses? Am I to travel with six white
horses and silver bells, or trudge on foot with
a wallet?"

"But you know quite well," said Mrs. Lorraine, warmly—"you know you will not touch
that money that Mrs. Lavender has left you."

"Oh, pardon me," he said; "I should rejoice
to have it if it did not properly belong to
someone else. And the difficulty is that Mr.
Mackenzie is obviously very anxious that neither
Mr. Lavender nor Sheila should have it. If
Sheila gets it, of course she will give it to her
husband. Now, if it is not to be given to
her, do you think I should regard the money
with any particular horror, and refuse to touch
it? That would be very romantic, perhaps;
but I should be sorry, you know, to give my
friends the most disquieting doubts about my
sanity. Romance goes out of a man's head
when the hair gets grey."

"Until a man has grey hair," Mrs. Lorraine
said, still with some unnecessary fervour, "he
does not know that there are things much

more valuable than money. You wouldn't touch that money just now; and all the thinking and reasoning in the world will never get you to touch it."

"What am I to do with it?" he said, meekly.

"Give it to Mr. Mackenzie, in trust for his daughter," Mrs. Lorraine said, promptly; and then, seeing that her mother had gone to the end of the drawing-room, to fetch something or other, she added quickly: "I should be more sorry than I can tell you to find you accepting this money. You do not wish to have it. You do not need it. And if you did take it, it would prove a source of continual embarrassment and regret to you; and no assurances on the part of Mr. Mackenzie would be able to convince you that you had acted rightly by his daughter. Now, if you simply hand over your responsibilities to him, he cannot refuse them, for the sake of his own child, and you are left with the sense of having acted nobly and generously. I hope there are many men who would do what I ask you to do; but I have not met many to whom I could make such an appeal with any hope. But, after all, that is only advice. I have no right to ask you to do anything like that. You asked me for my opinion about it——Well, that is it. But I should not have asked you to act on it."

"But I will," he said, in a low voice; and then he went to the other end of the room, for Mrs. Kavanagh was calling him to help her in finding something she had lost.

Before he left, that evening, Mrs. Lorraine said to him—

"We go by the night mail to Paris to-morrow night; and we shall dine here at five. Would you have the courage to come up and join us in that melancholy ceremony?"

"Oh, yes," he said, "if I may go down to the station to see you away afterwards."

"I think if we got you so far, we should persuade you to go with us," Mrs. Kavanagh said, with a smile.

He sat silent for a minute. Of course, she could not seriously mean such a thing. But at all events she would not be displeased if he crossed their path while they were actually abroad.

"It is getting too late in the year to go to Scotland now," he said, with some hesitation.

"Oh, most certainly," Mrs. Lorraine said.

"I don't know where the man in whose yacht I was to have gone may be now. I might spend half my holiday in trying to catch him."

"And during that time you would be alone," Mrs. Lorraine said.

"I suppose the Tyrol is a very nice place," he suggested.

"Oh, most delightful," she exclaimed. "You know, we should go round by Switzerland, and go up by Lucerne and Zurich to the end of the Lake of Constance——Bregenz, Mamma, isn't that the place where we hired that good-natured man the year before last?"

"Yes, child."

"Now, you see, Mr. Ingram, if you had less time than we—if you could not start with us to-morrow—you might come straight down by Schaffhausen and the steamer, and catch us up there, and then Mamma would become your guide. I am sure we should have some pleasant days together, till you got tired of us, and then you could go off on a walking tour if you pleased. And then, you know, there would be no difficulty about our meeting at Bregenz; for Mamma and I have plenty of time, and we should wait there for a few days so as to make sure——"

"Cecilia," said Mrs. Kavanagh, "you must not persuade Mr. Ingram against his will. He may have other duties—other friends to see perhaps."

"Who proposed it, mamma?" said the daughter, calmly.

"I did, as a mere joke. But, of course, if Mr. Ingram thinks of going to the Tyrol, we should be most pleased to see him there."

"Oh, I have no other friends whom I am bound to see," Ingram said, with some hesitation; "and I should like to go to the Tyrol. But—the fact is—I am afraid --- "

"May I interrupt you?" said Mrs. Lorraine. "You do not like to leave London so long as your friend Sheila is in trouble. Is not that the case? And yet she has her father to look after her. And it is clear you cannot do much for her when you do not even know where Mr. Lavender is. On the whole, I think you should consider yourself a little bit now, and not get cheated out of your holidays for the year."

"Very well," Ingram said, "I shall be able to tell you to-morrow."

To be so phlegmatic and matter-of-fact a person, Mr. Ingram was sorely disturbed on going home that evening, nor did he sleep much during the night. For the more that he speculated on all the possibilities that might arise from his meeting those people in the Tyrol, the more pertinaciously did this refrain follow these excursive fancies—"*If I go to the Tyrol, I shall fall in love with that girl and ask her to marry me. And if I do so, what position should I hold with regard to her, as a penniless man with a rich wife?"*

He did not look at the question in such a light as the opinion of the world might throw on it. The difficulty was what she herself might afterwards come to think of their mutual relations. True it was that no one could be more gentle and submissive to him than she appeared to be. In matters of opinion and discussion he already ruled with an autocratic authority which he fully perceived himself, and exercised, too, with some sort of notion that it was good for this clear-headed young woman to have to submit to control. But of what avail would this moral authority be as against the consciousness she would have that it was her fortune that was supplying both with the means of living?

He went down to his office in the morning with no plans formed. The forenoon passed; and he had decided on nothing. At mid-day he suddenly bethought him that it would be very pleasant if Sheila would go and see Mrs. Lorraine; and forthwith he did that which would have driven Frank Lavender out of his senses —he telegraphed to Mrs. Lorraine for permission to bring Sheila and her father to dinner at five. He certainly knew that such a request was a trifle cool ; but he had discovered that Mrs. Lorraine was not easily shocked by such audacious experiments on her good-nature. When he received the telegram in reply, he knew it granted what he asked. The words were merely " Certainly—by all means—but not later than five."

Then he hastened down to the house in which Sheila lived, and found that she and her father had just returned from visiting some exhibition. Mr. Mackenzie was not in the room.

" Sheila," Ingram said, " what would you think of my getting married ?"

Sheila looked up with a bright smile and said—

" It would please me very much—it would be a great pleasure to me ; and I have expected it for some time."

" You have expected it ?" he repeated, with a stare.

" Yes," she said, quietly.

" Then you fancy you know——" he said, or rather stammered, in great embarrassment, when she interrupted him by saying—

" Oh, yes, I think I know. When you came down every evening to tell me all the praises of Mrs. Lorraine, and how clever she was, and

kind, I expected you would come some day
with another message; and now I am very glad
to hear it; you have changed all my opinions
about her, and——"

Then she rose and took both his hands, and
looked frankly into his face.

"——And I do hope most sincerely you will
be happy, my dear friend."

Ingram was fairly taken aback at the conse-
quences of his own imprudence. He had never
dreamed for a moment that anyone would have
suspected such a thing; and he had thrown out
the suggestion to Sheila almost as a jest, believ-
ing, of course, that it compromised no one. And
here—before he had spoken a word to Mrs.
Lorraine on the subject—he was being con-
gratulated on his approaching marriage.

"Oh, Sheila," he said, "this is all a mistake.
It was a joke of mine—if I had known you
would think of Mrs. Lorraine, I should not have
said a word about it——"

"But it is Mrs. Lorraine?" Sheila said.

"Well, but I have never mentioned such a
thing to her—never hinted it in the remotest·
manner. I dare say if I had, she might laugh
the matter aside as too absurd."

"She will not do that," Sheila said; "if you
ask her to marry you, she will marry you. I

am sure of that from what I have heard, and she would be very foolish if she was not proud and glad to do that. And you—what doubt can you have, after all that you have been saying of late ?"

"But you don't marry a woman merely because you admire her cleverness and kindness," he said; and then he added suddenly, "Sheila, would you do me a great favour? Mrs. Lorraine and her mother are leaving for the continent to-night. They dine at five; and I am commissioned to ask you and your papa if you would go up with me and have some dinner with them, you know, before they start. Won't you do that, Sheila ?"

The girl shook her head, without answering. She had not gone to any friend's house since her husband had left London; and that house above all others was calculated to awaken in her bitter recollections.

"Won't you, Sheila ?" he said. "You used to go there. I know they like you very much. I have seen you very well pleased and comfortable there, and I thought you were enjoying yourself.'

"Yes, that is true," she said; and then she looked up, with a strange sort of smile on her lips, "but ' *what made the assembly shine ?* ' "

That forced smile did not last long: the girl

suddenly burst into tears, and rose, and went away to the window. Mackenzie came into the room; he did not see his daughter was crying.

"Well, Mr. Ingram, and are you coming with us to Lewis? We cannot always be staying in London, for there will be many things wanting the looking after in Borva, as you will know ferry well. And yet Sheila she will not go back; and Mairi, too, she will be forgetting the ferry sight of her own people; but if you wass coming with us, Mr. Ingram, Sheila she would come too, and it would be ferry good for her whatever."

"I have brought you another proposal. Will you take Sheila to see the Tyrol, and I will go with you?"

"The Tyrol?" said Mr. Mackenzie. "Ay, it is a ferry long way away, but if Sheila will care to go to the Tyrol—oh, yes! I will go to the Tyrol, or anywhere if she will go out of London, for it is not good for a young girl to be always in the one house, and no company, and no variety; and I wass saying to Sheila what good will she do sitting by the window, and thinking over things, and crying sometimes—by Kott, it is a foolish thing for a young girl, and I will hef no more of it!"

In other circumstances Ingram would have laughed at this dreadful threat. Despite the frown on the old man's face, the sudden stamp of his foot, and the vehemence of his words, Ingram knew that if Sheila had turned round and said that she wished to be shut up in a dark room for the rest of her life, the old King of Borva would have said, "Ferry well, Sheila," in the meekest way, and would have been satisfied if only he could share her imprisonment with her.

"But first of all, Mr. Mackenzie, I have another proposal to make to you," Ingram said; and then he urged upon Sheila's father to accept Mrs. Lorraine's invitation. Mr. Mackenzie was nothing loth; Sheila was living by far too monotonous a life. He went over to the window to her and said—

"Sheila, my lass, you wass going nowhere else this evening; and it would be ferry convenient to go with Mr. Ingram, and he would see his friends away, and we could go to a theatre then. And it is no new thing for you to go to fine houses, and see other people; but it is new to me, and you wass saying what a beautiful house it wass many a time, and I hef wished to see it. And the people they are ferry kind, Sheila, to send me an invitation, and if they wass to come to the Lewis, what would you think if you asked them to come to your house, and they paid no heed to it ? Now, it is after four, Sheila, and if you wass to get ready now——"

"Yes, I will go and get ready, papa," she said.

Ingram had a vague consciousness that he was taking Sheila up to introduce to her Mrs. Lorraine in a new character. Would Sheila look at the woman she used to fear and dislike in a wholly different fashion, and be prepared to adorn her with all the graces which he had so often described to her ? Ingram hoped that Sheila would get to like Mrs. Lorraine; and that by-and-by a better acquaintance between them might lead to a warm and friendly intimacy. Somehow he felt that if Sheila would betray such a liking—if she would come to him and say honestly that she was rejoiced he meant to marry —all his doubts would be cleared away. Sheila had already said pretty nearly as much as that ; but then it followed what she understood to be an announcement of his approaching marriage, and, of course, the girl's kindly nature at once suggested a few pretty speeches. Sheila now knew that nothing was settled ; after looking at Mrs. Lorraine in the light of these new possibilities, would she come to him and council him to go on and challenge a decision ?

Mr. Mackenzie received with a grave dignity

and politeness the more than friendly welcome
given him both by Mrs. Kavanagh and her
daughter; and, in view of their approaching
tour, he gave them to understand that he had
himself established somewhat familiar relations
with foreign countries by reason of his meeting
with the ships and sailors hailing from these
distant shores.   He displayed a profound knowledge of the habits and customs, and of the
natural products, of many remote lands, which
were much further afield than a little bit of in-
land Germany.   He represented the island of
Borva, indeed, as a sort of lighthouse from which
you could survey pretty nearly all the countries
of the globe; and broadly hinted that, so far
from insular prejudice being the fruit of living in
such a place, a general intercourse with diverse
peoples tended to widen the understanding and
throw light on the various social experiments that
had been made by the lawgivers, the philan-
thropists, the philosophers of the world.

It seemed to Sheila, as she sat and listened,
that the pale, calm, and clear-eyed young lady
opposite her was not quite so self-possessed as
usual.   She seemed shy, and a little self-conscious.
Did she suspect that she was being observed,
Sheila wondered; and the reason?   When
dinner was announced she took Sheila's arm, and

allowed Mr. Ingram to follow them, protesting,
into the other room ; but there was much more
of embarrassment and timidity than of an
audacious mischief in her look. She was very
kind indeed to Sheila ; but she had wholly
abandoned that air of maternal patronage which
she used to assume towards the girl. She
seemed to wish to be more friendly and confidential with her ; and, indeed, scarcely spoke a
word to Ingram during dinner, so persistently
did she talk to Sheila, who sat next her.

Ingram got vexed.

"Mrs. Lorraine," he said, "you seem to forget
that this is a solemn occasion. You ask us to a
farewell banquet ; but instead of observing the
proper ceremonies, you pass the time in talking
about fancy-work, and music, and other ordinary
every-day trifles."

" What are the ceremonies ? " she said.

" Well," he answered, " you need not occupy
the time with crochet——"

" Mrs. Lavender and I are very well pleased
to talk about trifles."

" But I am not," he said, bluntly, " and I am
not going to be shut out by a conspiracy. Come,
let us talk about your journey."

" Will my lord give his commands as to the
point at which we shall start the conversation."

" You may skip the Channel."

" I wish I could," she remarked with a sigh.

" We shall land you in Paris. How are we to know that you have arrived safely ? "

She looked embarrassed for a moment, and then said—

" If it is of any consequence for you to know, I shall be writing in any case to Mrs. Lavender, about some little private matter."

Ingram did not receive this promise with any great show of delight.

" You see," he said, somewhat glumly, " if I am to meet you anywhere, I should like to know the various stages of your route, so that I could guard against our missing each other."

" You have decided to go then ? "

Ingram, not looking at her, but looking at Sheila, said " Yes ! " and Sheila, despite all her efforts, could not help glancing up with a brief smile and blush of pleasure that were quite visible to everybody. Mrs. Lorraine struck in, with a sort of nervous haste,—

" Oh, that will be very pleasant for mamma ; for she gets rather tired of me at times when we are travelling. Two women who always read the same sort of books, and have the same opinions about the people they meet, and have precisely the same tastes in everything, are not very amusing companions for each other. You want a little discussion thrown in——"

" And if we meet Mr. Ingram we are sure to have that," Mrs. Kavanagh said, benignly.

" And you want somebody to give you new opinions, and put things differently, you know. I am sure mamma will be most kind to you, if you can make it convenient to spend a few days with us, Mr. Ingram."

" And I have been trying to persuade Mr. Mackenzie and this young lady to come also," said Ingram.

" Oh, that would be delightful ! " Mrs. Lorraine cried, suddenly taking Sheila's hand. " You will come, won't you ? We should have such a pleasant party. I am sure your papa would be most interested ; and we are not tied to any route—we should go wherever you pleased."

She would have gone on beseeching and advising, but she saw something in Sheila's face which told her that all her efforts would be unavailing.

" It is very kind of you," Sheila said, " but I do not think I can go to the Tyrol."

" Then you will go back to the Lewis, Sheila," her father said.

" I cannot go back to the Lewis, papa," she

said, simply ; and at this point Ingram, per-
ceiving how painful the discussion was for the
girl, suddenly called attention to the hour, and
asked Mrs. Kavanagh if all her portmanteaus
were strapped up.

They drove in a body down to the station ;
and Mr. Ingram was most assiduous in supplying the two travellers with an abundance of
everything they could not possibly want. He
got them a reading-lamp, though both of them
declared they never read in a train. He got
them some eau-de-cologne, though they had
plenty in their travelling case. He purchased for
them an amount of miscellaneous literature that
would have been of benefit to a hospital—provided that the patients were strong enough to
bear it. And then bade them good-bye at least
half-a-dozen times as the train was slowly moving out of the station, and made the most solemn
vows about meeting them at Bregenz.

"Now, Sheila," he said, "shall we go to a
theatre ? "

"I do not care to go unless you wish," was
the answer.

"She does not care to go anywhere now,"
her father said ; and then the girl, seeing that
he was rather distressed about her apparent

want of interest, pulled herself together and said, cheerfully—

"Is it not too late to go to a theatre? And I am sure we could be very comfortable at home. Mairi, she will think it very unkind if we go to the theatre by ourselves."

"Mairi!" said her father, impatiently, for he never lost an opportunity of indirectly justifying Lavender. "Mairi has more sense than you, Sheila, and she knows that a servant-lass has to stay at home, and she knows that she is ferry different from you, and she is a ferry good girl whatever, and hass no pride, and she does not expect nonsense in going about and such things."

"I am quite sure, papa, you would rather go home and sit down and have a talk with Mr. Ingram, and a pipe, and a little whisky, than go to any theatre."

"What I would do! And what I would like!" said her father, in a vexed way. "Sheila you have no more sense as a lass that wass still at the school. I want you to go to the theatre, and amuse yourself, instead of sitting in the house, and thinking, thinking, thinking. And all for what?"

"But if one has something to be sorry for, is it not better to think of it?"

"And what hef *you* to be sorry for?" said her father, in amazement, and forgetting that, in his diplomatic fashion, he had been accustoming Sheila to the notion that she, too, might have erred grievously and been in part responsible for all that had occurred.

"I have a great deal to be sorry for, papa," she said; and then she renewed her entreaties that her two companions should abandon their notion of going to a theatre, and resolved to spend the rest of the evening in what she consented to call her home.

After all they formed a comfortable little company when they sat round the fire, which had been lit for cheerfulness rather than for warmth; and Ingram, at least, was in a particularly pleasant mood. For Sheila had seized the opportunity, when her father had gone out of the room for a few minutes, to say, suddenly—

"Oh, my dear friend, if you care for her, you have a great happiness before you."

"Why, Sheila?" he said, staring.

"She cares for you more than you can think—I saw it to-night in everything she said and did."

"I thought she was just a trifle saucy, do you know. She shunted me out of the conversation altogether."

Sheila shook her head and smiled.

" She was embarrassed. She suspects that you like her, and that I know it, and that I came to see her. If you ask her to marry you, she will do it gladly."

" Sheila," Ingram said, with a severity that was not in his heart, " you must not say such things. You might make fearful mischief by putting these wild notions into people's heads."

" They are not wild notions," she said, quietly. " A woman can tell what another woman is thinking about better than a man."

" And am I to go to the Tyrol and ask her to marry me ?" he said, with the air of a meek scholar.

" I should like to see you married—very, very much indeed," Sheila said.

" And to her ? "

" Yes, to her," the girl said, frankly. " For I am sure she has a great regard for you, and she is clever enough to put value on—on—but I cannot flatter you, Mr. Ingram."

" Shall I send you word about what happens in the Tyrol ? " he said, still with the humble air of one receiving instructions.

" Yes."

" And if she rejects me, what shall I do ? "

" She will not reject you."

"Shall I come to you for consolation, and ask you what you meant by driving me on such a blunder?"

"If she rejects you," Sheila said, with a smile, "it will be your own fault, and you will deserve it. For you are a little too harsh with her, and you have too much authority, and I am surprised that she will be so amiable under it. Because, you know, a woman expects to be treated with much gentleness and deference before she has said she will marry—she likes to be entreated, and coaxed, and made much of; but instead of that, you are very overbearing with Mrs. Lorraine."

"I did not mean to be, Sheila," he said, honestly enough. "If anything of the kind happened, it must have been in a joke."

"Oh no, not a joke," Sheila said; "and I have noticed it before—the very first evening you came to their house. And perhaps you did not know of it yourself; and then Mrs. Lorraine, she is clever enough to see that you did not mean to be disrespectful. But she will expect you to alter that a great deal if you ask her to marry you—that is, until you are married."

"Have I ever been overbearing to you, Sheila?" he asked.

"To me? Oh, no. You have always been

very gentle to me; but I know how that is.
When you first knew me, I was almost a child,
and you treated me like a child; and ever since
then it has always been the same. But to
others—yes, you are too unceremonious; and
Mrs. Lorraine will expect you to be much more
mild and amiable, and you must let her have
opinions of her own——"

"Sheila, you give me to understand that I am
a bear," he said, in tones of injured protest.

Sheila laughed.

"Have I told you the truth at last? It was
no matter as long as you had ordinary acquaintances to deal with. But now, if you wish to
marry that pretty lady, you must be much more
gentle if you are discussing anything with her;
and if she says anything that is not very wise,
you must not say bluntly that it is foolish, but
you must smooth it away, and put her right
gently, and then she will be grateful to you.
But if you say to her, 'Oh, that is nonsense,'
as you might say to a man, you will hurt her
very much. The man would not care; he
would think you were stupid to have a different
opinion from him; but a woman fears she is
not as clever as the man she is talking to, and
likes his good opinion; and if he says something careless like that, she is sensitive to it, and

it wounds her. To-night you contradicted Mrs. Lorraine about the *h* in those Italian words; and I am quite sure you were wrong. She knows Italian much better than you do; and yet she yielded to you very prettily."

" Go on, Sheila; go on," he said, with a resigned air. " What else did I do?"

" Oh, a great many rude things. You should not have contradicted Mrs. Kavanagh about the colour of an amethyst!"

" But why? You know she was wrong; and she said herself a minute afterwards that she was thinking of a sapphire."

" But you ought not to contradict a person older than yourself," said Sheila, sententiously.

" Goodness gracious me! Because one person is born in one year, and one in another, is that any reason why you should say that an amethyst is blue? Mr. Mackenzie, come and talk to this girl. She is trying to pervert my principles. She says that in talking to a woman you have to abandon all hope of being accurate, and that respect for the truth is not to be thought of. Because a woman has a pretty face she is to be allowed to say that black is white, and white pea-green. And if you say anything to the contrary, you are a brute, and had better go and bellow by yourself in a wilderness."

"Sheila is quite right," said old Mackenzie, at a venture.

"Oh, do you think so?" Ingram asked, coolly. "Then I can understand how her moral sentiment has been destroyed; and it is easy to see where she has got a set of opinions that strike at the very roots of a respectable and decent society."

"Do you know," said Sheila, seriously, "that it is very rude of you to say so, even in jest? If you treat Mrs. Lorraine in this way——"

She suddenly stopped. Her father had not heard, being busy among his pipes. So the subject was discreetly dropped, Ingram reluctantly promising to pay some attention to Sheila's precepts of politeness.

Altogether, it was a pleasant evening they had; but when Ingram had left, Mr. Mackenzie said to his daughter—

"Now, look at this, Sheila. When Mr. Ingram goes away from London, you hef no friend at all then in the place, and you are quite alone. Why will you not come to the Lewis, Sheila? It is no one there will know anything of what has happened here; and Mairi she is a good girl, and she will hold her tongue."

"They will ask me why I come back without my husband," Sheila said, looking down.

"Oh, you will leave that all to me," said her
father, who knew he had surely sufficient skill to
thwart the curiosity of a few simple creatures in
Borva. "There is many a girl hass to go home
for a time, while her husband he is away on his
business; and there will no one hef the right to
ask you any more than I will tell them, and I
will tell them what they should know—oh, yes,
I will tell them ferry well, and you will hef no
trouble about it. And Sheila, you are a good
lass, and you know that I hef many things to
attend to that is not easy to write about——"

"I do know that, Papa," the girl said, "and
many a time have I wished you would go back
to the Lewis."

"And leave you here by yourself? Why, you
are talking foolishly, Sheila. But now, Sheila,
you will see how you could go back with me,
and it would be a ferry different thing for you
running about in the fresh air than shut up in a
room in the middle of a town. And you are
not looking ferry well, my lass, and Scarlett she
will hef to take the charge of you."

"I will go to the Lewis with you, Papa, when
you please," she said; and he was glad and proud
to hear her decision; but there was no happy
light of anticipation in her eyes, such as ought
to have been awakened by this projected journey

to the far island which she had known as her
home.

And so it was, that one rough and blustering
afternoon the *Clansman* steamed into Stornoway
harbour; and Sheila, casting timid and furtive
glances towards the quay, saw Duncan standing
there, with the waggonette some little distance
back, under charge of a boy. Duncan was a
proud man that day. He was the first to shove
the gangway on to the vessel, and he was the
first to get on board; and in another minute
Sheila found the tall, keen-eyed, brown-faced
keeper before her, and he was talking in a rapid
and eager fashion, throwing in an occasional
scrap of Gaelic in the mere hurry of his words.

"Oh yes, Miss Sheila, Scarlett she is ferry
well whatever, but there is nothing will make
her so well as your coming back to sa Lewis,
and we wass saying yesterday that it looked as
if it wass more as three or four years, or six
years, since you went away from sa Lewis, but
now it iss no time at all, for you are just the
same Miss Sheila as we knew before; and there
is not one in all Borva but will think it iss a
good day this day that you will come back——"

"Duncan!" said Mackenzie, with an impatient stamp of his foot, "why will you talk
like a foolish man? Get the luggage to the

shore, instead of keeping us all the day in the boat."

"Oh, ferry well, Mr. Mackenzie," said Duncan, departing with an injured air, and grumbling as he went; "it iss no new thing to you to see Miss Sheila, and you will have no thocht for anyone but yourself. But I will get out the luggage— oh, yes; I will get out the luggage."

Sheila, in truth, had but little luggage with her; but she remained on board the boat until Duncan was quite ready to start, for she did not wish just then to meet any of her friends in Stornoway. Then she stepped ashore, and crossed the quay, and got into the waggonette; and the two horses, whom she had caressed for a moment, seemed to know that they were carrying Sheila back to her own country, from the speed with which they rattled out of the town, and away into the lonely moorland.

Mackenzie let them have their way. Past the solitary lakes they went, past the long stretches of undulating morass, past the lonely sheilings perched far up on the hills; and the rough and blustering wind blew about them, and the grey clouds hurried by, and the old, strong-bearded man who shook the reins and gave the horses their heads, could have laughed aloud in his joy that he was driving his daughter home. But

Sheila—she sat there as one dead; and Mairi, timidly regarding her, wondered what the impassible face and the bewildered, sad eyes meant. Did she not smell the sweet strong scent of the heather? Had she no interest in the great birds that were circling in the air over by the Barbhas mountains? Where was the pleasure she used to exhibit in remembering the curious names of the small lakes they passed?

And lo! the rough grey day broke asunder, and a great blaze of fire appeared in the west, shining across the moors and touching the blue slopes of the distant hills. Sheila was getting near to the region of beautiful sunsets and lambent twilights, and the constant movement and mystery of the sea. Overhead the heavy clouds were still hurried on by the wind; and in the south the eastern slopes of the hills and the moors were getting to be of a soft purple; but all along the west, where her home was, lay a great flush of gold, and she knew that Loch Roag was shining there, and the gable of the house at Borvabost getting warm in the beautiful light.

"It is a good afternoon you will be getting to see Borva again," her father said to her; but all the answer she made was to ask her father not to stop at Garra-na-hina, but to drive straight

on to Callernish. She would visit the people at
Garra-na-hina some other day.

The boat was waiting for them at Callernish,
and the boat was the *Maighdean-mhara.*

"How pretty she is! How have you kept
her so well, Duncan?" said Sheila, her face
lighting up for the first time, as she went down
the path to the bright-painted little vessel that
scarcely rocked in the water below.

"Bekass we neffer knew but that it was this
week, or the week before, or the next week you
would come back, Miss Sheila, and you would
want your boat; but it wass Mr. Mackenzie
himself, it wass he that did all the pentin of the
boat, and it iss as well done as Mr. McNicol
could have done it, and a great deal better than
that mirover."

"Won't you steer her yourself, Sheila?" her
father suggested, glad to see that she was at
last being interested and pleased.

"Oh, yes; I will steer her, if I have not
forgotten all the points that Duncan taught
me."

"And I am sure you hef not done that, Miss
Sheila," Duncan said; "for there wass no one
knew Loch Roag better as you, not one, and
you hef not been so long away; and when you
tek the tiller in your hand, it will all come back

to you just as if you wass going away from Borva the day before yesterday."

She certainly had not forgotten; and she was proud and pleased to see how well the shapely little craft performed its duties. They had a favourable wind, and ran rapidly along the opening channels, until, in due course, they glided into the well-known bay over which, and shining in the yellow light from the sunset, they saw Sheila's house.

She had escaped so far the trouble of meeting friends; but she could not escape her friends in Borvabost. They had waited for her for hours, not knowing when the *Clansman* might arrive at Stornoway; and now they crowded down to the shore, and there was a great shaking of hands, and an occasional sob from some old crone, and a thousand repetitions of the familiar "And are you ferry well, Miss Sheila?" from small children who had come across from the village in defiance of mothers and fathers. And Sheila's face brightened into a wonderful gladness, and she had a hundred questions to ask for one answer she got, and she did not know what to do with the number of small brown fists that wanted to shake hands with her.

"Will you let Miss Sheila alone?" Duncan called out, adding something in Gaelic which came strangely from a man who sometimes reproved his own master for swearing. "Get away with you, you brats; it wass better you would be in your beds than bothering people that wass come all the way from Styornoway."

Then they all went up in a body to the house; and Scarlett, who had neither eyes, ears, nor hands but for the young girl who had been the very pride of her heart, was nigh driven to distraction by Mackenzie's stormy demands for oatcake, and glasses, and whisky. Scarlett angrily remonstrated with her husband for allowing this rabble of people to interfere with the comfort of Miss Sheila; and Duncan, taking her reproaches with great good-humour, contented himself with doing her work, and went and got the cheese, and the plates, and the whisky, while Scarlett, with a hundred endearing phrases, was helping Sheila to take off her travelling things. And Sheila, it turned out, had brought with her in her portmanteau certain huge and wonderful cakes, not of oatmeal, from Glasgow; and these were soon on the great table in the kitchen, and Sheila herself distributing pieces to those small folks who were so awe-stricken by the sight of this strange dainty, that they forgot her injunctions and thanked her timidly in Gaelic.

"Well, Sheila, my lass," said her father to her,

as they stood at the door of the house and
watched the troop of their friends, children and
all, go over the hill to Borvabost, in the red light
of the sunset, "and are you glad to be home
again ? "

"Oh, yes," she said, heartily enough ; and
Mackenzie thought that things were going on
favourably.

"You hef no such sunsets in the South,
Sheila," he observed, loftily casting his eye
around, although he did not usually pay much
attention to the picturesqueness of his native
island ; " now look at the light there iss on
Suainabhal. Do you see the red on the water
down there, Sheila ? Oh yes, I thought you
would say it was ferry beautiful—it is a ferry
good colour on the water. The water looks
ferry well when it is red. You hef no such
things in London—not any, Sheila. Now we
must go indoors ; for these things you can see
any day here, and we must not keep our friends
waiting."

An ordinary, dull-witted, or careless man
might have been glad to have a little quiet after
so long and tedious a journey ; but Mr. Mackenzie was no such person. He had resolved to
guard against Sheila's first evening at home
being in any way languid or monotonous ; and

so he had asked one or two of his especial friends to remain and have supper with them. Moreover, he did not wish the girl to spend the rest of the evening out-of-doors, when the melancholy time of the twilight drew over the hills, and the sea began to sound remote and sad. Sheila should have a comfortable evening indoors; and he would himself, after supper, when the small parlour was well lit up, sing for her one or two songs, just to keep the thing going, as it were. He would let nobody else sing. These Gaelic songs were not the sort of music to make people cheerful. And if Sheila herself would sing for them?

And Sheila did. And her father chose the songs for her, and they were the blithest he could find, and the girl seemed really in excellent spirits. They had their pipes and their hot whisky and water in this little parlour; Mr. Mackenzie explaining that although his daughter was accustomed to spacious and gilded drawing-rooms where such a thing was impossible, she would do anything to make her friends welcome and comfortable, and they might fill their glasses and their pipes with impunity. And Sheila sang again and again, all cheerful and sensible English songs; and she listened to the odd jokes and stories her friends had to tell her; and Mackenzie was delighted with the success of his plans and precautions. Was not her very appearance now a triumph? She was laughing, smiling, talking to everyone; he had not seen her so happy for many a day.

In the midst of it all, when the night had come on apace, what was this wild skirl outside that made everybody start? Mackenzie jumped to his feet, with an angry vow in his heart, that if this "teffle of a piper John" should come down the hill playing "Lochaber no more" or "Cha till mi tuilich," or any other mournful tune, he would have his chanter broken in a thousand splinters over his head. But what was the wild air that came nearer and nearer, until John marched into the house, and came, with ribbons and pipes, to the very door of the room which was flung open to him? Not a very appropriate air, perhaps, for it was—

> " *The Campbells are coming, oho! oho!*
> *The Campbells are coming, oho! oho!*
> *The Campbells are coming to bonny Lochleven!*
> *The Campbells are coming, oho! oho!*"

but it was, to Mr. Mackenzie's rare delight, a right good joyous tune, and it was meant as a welcome to Sheila, and forthwith he caught the white-haired piper by the shoulder, and dragged him in, and said—

"Put down your pipes and come into the house, John! Put down your pipes, and tek off your bonnet, and we shall hef a good dram together this night, by Kott! And it is Sheila herself will pour out the whisky for you, John; and she is a good Highland girl, and she knows the piper was never born that could be hurt by whisky, and the whisky was neffer yet made that could hurt a piper. What do you say to that, John?"

John did not answer; he was standing before Sheila, with his bonnet in his hand, but with his pipes still proudly over his shoulder. And he took the glass from her, and called out "Shlainte!" and drained every drop of it out to welcome Mackenzie's daughter home.

CHAPTER VII.

THE VOYAGE OF THE "PHŒBE."

IT was a cold morning in January, and up here
among the Jura hills the clouds had melted into
a small and chilling rain that fell ceaselessly.
The great "Paps of Jura" were hidden in the
mist; even the valleys near at hand were vague,
and dismal in the pale fog; and the Sound of
Islay, lying below, and the far sea beyond, were
gradually growing indistinguishable. In a rude
little sheiling, built on one of the plateaus of
rock, Frank Lavender sat alone, listening to the
plashing of the rain without. A rifle that he
had just carefully dried lay across his knees.
A brace of deerhounds had stretched out their
paws on the earthen floor, and had put their long
noses between their paws to produce a little
warmth. It was, indeed, a cold and damp
morning; and the little hut was pervaded with
a smell of wet wood, and also of peat-ashes, for

one of the gillies had tried to light a fire, but the peats had gone out.

It was Lavender who had let the fire go out He had forgotten it. He was thinking of other things—of a song, mostly, that Sheila used to sing; and lines of it went hither and thither through his brain, as he recalled the sound of her voice :—

> " *Haste to thy barque,*
> *Coastwise steer not ;*
> *Sail wide of Mull,*
> *Jura near not !*

> " *Farewell, she said,*
> *Her last pang subduing,*
> *Brave Mac Intyre,*
> *Costly thy wooing !* "

There came into the sheiling a little wiry old keeper, with shaggy grey hair and keen black eyes.

"Cosh bless me!" he said, petulantly, as he wrung the rain out of his bonnet, "you hef let the peats go out, Mr. Lavender, and who will tell when the rain will go off?"

"It can't last long, Neil. It came on too suddenly for that. I thought we were going to get one fine day when we started this morning; but you don't often manage that here, Neil."

"Indeed no, sir," said Neil, who was not a
native of Jura, and was as eager as anyone to
abuse the weather prevailing there; "it is a
ferry bad place for the weather. If the Almichty
were to tek the sun away a' tagether, it would
be days and weeks and days before you would find
it oot. But it iss a good thing, sir, you will get the
one stag before the mist came down; and he is
not a stag, mirover, but a fine big hart, and a
royal, too, and I hef not seen many finer in the
Jura hills. Oh, yes, sir, when he was crossing
the burn, I made out his points ferry well, and I
wass saying to myself, 'Now, if Mr. Lavender
will get this one, it will be a grand day this
day, and it will make up for many a wet day
among the hills.' "

"They haven't come back with the pony
yet?" Lavender asked, laying down his gun
and going to the door of the hut.

"Oh no," Neil said, following him, "it iss a
long way to get the powny, and maybe they
will stop at Mr. MacDougall's to hef a dram.
And Mr. MacDougall was saying to me yesterday that the ferry next time you wass shoot a
royal, he would have the horns dressed and the
head stuffed to make you a present, for he is
ferry proud of the picture of Miss Margaret, and
he will say to me many's sa time that I wass to

gif you the ferry best shooting, and not to be afraid of disturbing sa deer, when you had a mind to go out. And I am not sure, sir, we will not get another stag to tek down with us yet, if the wind would carry away the mist, for the rain that is nearly off now, and as you are very wet, sir, already, it is no matter if we go down through the glen and cross the water to get the side of Ben Bheulah."

"That is true enough, Neil; and I fancy the clouds are beginning to lift. And there they come with the pony."

Neil directed his glass towards a small group that appeared to be coming up the side of the valley below them, and that was still at some considerable distance.

"Cosh bless me!" he cried, "what is that? There iss two strangers—oh yes, indeed, and mirover and there is one of them on the pony."

Lavender's heart leaped within him. If they were strangers, they were coming to see him; and how long was it since he had seen the face of any one of his old friends and companions? It seemed to him years.

"Is it a man or a woman on the pony, Neil?" he asked, hurriedly, with some wild fancy flashing through his brain. "Give me the glass!"

"Oh, it is a man," said Neil, handing over the glass. "What would a woman be doing up sa hills on a morning like this?"

The small party below came up out of the grey mist; and Lavender in the distance heard a long view-halloo.

"Cott tam them!" said Neil, at a venture. "There is not a deer on Benan Cabrach that will not hear them!"

"But if these strangers are coming to see me, I fear we must leave the deer alone, Neil."

"Ferry well, sir, ferry well, sir, it is a bad day whatever; and it is not many strangers will come to Jura. I suppose they hef come to Port Ascaig, and taken the ferry across the Sound."

"I am going to meet them on chance," Lavender said, and he set off along the side of the deep valley, leaving Neil with the dogs and the rifles.

"Hillo, Johnny!" he cried, in amazement, when he came upon the advancing group. "And you, Mosenberg! By Jove, how did you ever get here?"

There was an abundance of hand-shaking and incoherent questions when young Mosenberg jumped down on the wet heather, and the three friends bad actually met. Lavender scarcely

knew what to say : these two faces were so
strange, and yet so familiar ; their appearance
there was so unexpected, his pleasure so great.

"I can't believe my eyes yet, Johnny. Why
did you bring him here? Don't you know
what you'll have to put up with in this place.
Well, this does do a fellow's heart good. I am
awfully pleased to see you, and it is very kind
of you——"

"But I am very cold," the handsome Jew-boy
said, swinging his arms and stamping his feet.
"Wet boots, wet carts, wet roads, wet saddles,
and everywhere cold, cold, cold——"

"And he won't drink whisky, so what is be
to expect ?" Johnny Eyre said.

"Come along up to a little hut here," Lavender said, "and we'll try to get a fire lit. And
I have some brandy there——"

"And you have plenty of water to mix with
it," said the boy, looking mournfully around.
"Very good. Let us have the fire and the
warm drink ; and then, you know the story of
the music that was frozen in the trumpet, and
that all came out when it was thawed at a fire ?
When we get warm we have very great news to
tell you—oh, very great news indeed."

"I don't want any news—I want your company. Come along, like good fellows, and

leave the news for afterwards. The men are going on with a pony to fetch a stag that has been shot—they won't be back for an hour, I suppose, at the soonest. This is the sheiling up here, where the brandy is secreted. Now, Neil, help us to get up a blaze. If any of you have newspapers, letters, or anything that will set a few sticks on fire——"

"I have a box of wax matches," Johnny said, "and I know how to light a peat-fire better than any man in the country."

He was not very successful at first, for the peats were a trifle damp; but in the end he conquered, and a very fair blaze was produced, although the smoke that filled the sheiling had nearly blinded Mosenberg's eyes. Then Lavender produced a small tin pot and a solitary tumbler; and they boiled some water, and lit their pipes, and made themselves seats of peat round the fire. All the while a brisk conversation was going on, some portions of which astonished Lavender considerably.

For months back, indeed, he had almost cut himself off from the civilized world. His address was known to one or two persons; and sometimes they sent him a letter; but he was a bad correspondent. The news of his aunt's death did not reach him till a fortnight after the

funeral; and then it was by a singular chance
that he noticed it in the columns of an old
newspaper.

"That is the only thing I regret about coming
away," he was saying to these two friends of
his; "I should like to have seen the old woman
before she died. She was very kind to me."

"Well," said Johnny Eyre, with a shake of
the head, "that is all very well; but a mere
outsider like myself—you see it looks to me a
little unnatural that she should go and leave her
money to a mere friend, and not to her own
relations——"

"I am very glad she did," Lavender said.
"I had as good as asked her to do it long
before. And Ted Ingram will make a better
use of it than I ever did."

"It is all very well for you to say so now,
after all this fuss about those two pictures; but
suppose she had left you to starve?"

"Never mind suppositions," Lavender said,
to get rid of the subject. "Tell me, Mosenberg,
how is that overture of yours getting on?"

"It is nearly finished," said the lad, with
a flush of pleasure, "and I have shown it in
rough to two or three good friends, and—shall
I tell you?—it may be performed at the Crystal
Palace. But that is a chance. And the fate of

it, that is also a chance. But you—you have succeeded all at once, and brilliantly, and all the world is talking of you; and yet you go away among mountains, and live in the cold and wet, and you might as well be dead."

"What an ungrateful boy it is!" Lavender cried. "Here you have a comfortable fire, and hot brandy-and-water, and biscuits, and cigars if you wish; and you talk about people wishing to leave these things and die! Don't you know that in half-an-hour's time you will see that pony come back with a deer—a royal hart—slung across it; and won't you be proud when Mac-Dougall takes you out and gives you a chance of driving home such a prize? Then you will carry the horns back to London, and you will have them put up, and you will discourse to your friends of the span, and the pearls of the antlers, and the crockets? To-night after supper you will see the horns and the head brought into the room, and if you fancy that you your-self shot the stag, you will see that this life among the hills has its compensations."

"It is a very cold life," the lad said, passing his hands over the fire.

"That is because you won't drink anything," said Johnny Eyre, against whom no such charge could be brought. "And don't you know that the drinking of whisky is a provision invented by nature to guard human beings like you and me from cold and wet? You are flying in the face of Providence if you don't drink whisky among the Scotch hills."

"And have you people to talk to?" said Mosenberg, looking at Lavender with a vague wonder, for he could not understand why any man should choose such a life.

"Not many."

"What do you do on the long evenings when you are by yourself?"

"Well it isn't very cheerful; but it does a man good service sometimes to be alone for a time; it lets him find himself out."

"You ought to be up in London, to have all the praise of the people about your two pictures. Everyone is talking of them; the newspapers, too—have you seen the newspapers?"

"One or two. But all I know of these two pictures is derived from offers forwarded me by the Secretary at the Exhibition Rooms. I was surprised when I got them at first. But never mind them. Tell me more about the people one used to know. What about Ingram now? Has he cut the Board of Trade? Does he drive in the Park? Is he still in his rooms in Sloane Street?"

"Then you have had no letters from him?" Mosenberg said, with some surprise.

"No. Probably he does not know where I am. In any case——"

"But he is going to be married!" Mosenberg cried. "You did not know that? And to Mrs. Lorraine?"

"You don't say so! Why, he used to hate her—but that was before he knew her. To Mrs. Lorraine?"

"Yes. And it is amusing. She is so proud of him. And if he speaks at the table, she will turn away from you, as if you were not worth listening to, and have all her attention for him. And whatever is his opinion, she will defend that, and you must not disagree with her—oh, it is very amusing!" And the lad laughed, and shook back his curls.

"It is an odd thing," Lavender said; "but many a time, long before Ingram ever saw Mrs. Lorraine, I used to imagine these two married. I knew she was just the sort of clever, independent, clear-headed woman, to see Ingram's strong points, and rate them at their proper value. But I never expected anything of the sort, of course; for I had always a notion that some day or other he would be led into marrying some pretty, gentle, and soft-headed young thing,

whom he would have to take through life in a
protecting sort of way, and who would never
be a real companion for him. So he is
to marry Mrs. Lorraine, after all! Well, he
won't become a man of fashion, despite all his
money. He is sure to start a yacht, for one
thing. And they will travel a deal, I suppose.
I must write and congratulate him."

"I met him on the day I went to see your
picture," Mosenberg said. "Mrs. Lorraine was
looking at it a long time, and at last she came
back and said, 'The sea in that picture makes me
feel cold.' That was a compliment, was it not?
Only you cannot get a good view very often; for
the people will not stand back from the pictures.
But everyone asks why you did not keep these
two over for the Academy."

"I shall have other two for the Academy, I
hope."

"Commissions?" Johnny asked, with a practical air.

"No. I have had some offers; but I prefer
to leave the thing open. But you have not told
me how you got here yet," Lavender added,
continually breaking away from this subject of
the pictures.

"In the *Phœbe*," Eyre said.

"Is she in the bay?"

"Oh no.   We had to leave her at Port Ellen
to get a few small repairs done, and Mosenberg
and I came on by road to Port Ascaig.   Mind
you, she was quite small enough to come round
the Mull at this time of the year."

"I should think so.   What's your crew?"

"Two men and a lad, besides Mosenberg and
myself, and I can tell you we had our hands full
sometimes."

"You've given up open boats with stone
ballast now," Lavender said, with a laugh.

"Rather.   But it was no laughing matter,"
Eyre added, with a sudden gravity coming over
his face.   "It was the narrowest squeak I ever
had, and I don't know now how I clung on to
that place till the day broke.   When I came to
myself and called out for you, I never expected
to hear you answer; and in the darkness, by
Jove! your voice sounded like the voice of a
ghost.   How you managed to drag me so far up
that seaweed I can't imagine; and then the
dipping down and under the boat——"

"It was that dip down that saved me,"
Lavender said.   "It brought me to; and made
me scramble like a rat up the other side as soon
as I felt my hands on the rock again.   It was a
narrow squeak, as you say, Johnny.   Do you
remember how black the place looked when the

first light began to show in the sky; and how
we kept each other awake by calling; and how
you called 'hurrah!' when we heard Donald;
and how strange it was to find ourselves so near
the mouth of the harbour, after all? During the
night I fancied we must have been thrown on
Battie Island, you know——"

"I do not like to hear about that," young
Mosenberg said. "And always, if the wind
came on strong, or if the skies grew black, Eyre
would tell me all the story over again when we
were in this boat coming down by Arran and
Cantyre. Let us go out and see if they come
with the deer. Has the rain stopped?"

At this moment, indeed, sounds of the approaching party were heard, and when Lavender
and his friends went to the door, the pony, with
the deer slung on to him, was just coming up.
It was a sufficiently picturesque sight—the rude
little sheiling with its peat-fire, the brown and
wiry gillies, the slain deer roped on to the pony,
and all around the wild magnificence of hill and
valley clothed in moving mists. The rain had,
indeed, cleared off; but these pale white fogs
still clung around the mountains, and rendered
the valleys vague and shadowy. Lavender in-
formed Neil that he would make no further
effort that day; he gave the men a glass of

whisky all round ; and then, with his friends, he proceeded to make his way down to the small white cottage fronting the Sound of Islay, which had been his home for months back.

Just before setting off, however, he managed to take young Mosenberg aside for a moment.

" I suppose," he said, with his eyes cast down, " I suppose you heard something from Ingram of—of Sheila ? "

" Yes," said the lad, rather bashfully. " Ingram had heard from her. She was still in Lewis."

" And well ? "

" I think so ; yes," said Mosenberg ; and then he added, with some hesitation, " I should like to speak to you about it when we have the opportunity. There were some things that Mr. Ingram said—I am sure he would like you to know them."

" There was no message to me ? " Lavender asked, in a low voice.

" From her ? No. But it was the opinion of Mr. Ingram———"

" Oh, never mind that, Mosenberg," said the other, turning away wearily. " I suppose you won't find it too fatiguing to walk from here back ? It will warm you, you know ; and the old woman down there will get you something to eat.   You may make it luncheon or dinner, as you like, for it will be nearly two by the time you get down.   Then you can go for a prowl round the coast ; if it does not rain, I shall be working as long as there is daylight.   Then we can have a dinner and supper combined in the evening.   You will get venison and whisky."

" Don't you ever have anything else ? "

" Oh yes.   The venison will be in honour of you.   I generally have mutton and whisky."

" Look here, Lavender," the lad said, with considerable confusion, " the fact is—Eyre and I —we brought you a few things in the *Phœbe*— a little wine, you know, and some such things. To-morrow, if you could get a messenger to go down to Port Ellen—but no, I suppose we must go and work the boat up the Sound."

" If you do that, I must go with you," Lavender said, " for the chances are that your skipper doesn't know the currents in the Sound, and they are rather peculiar, I can tell you.   So Johnny and you have brought me some wine. I wish we had it now, to celebrate your arrival ; for I am afraid I can offer you nothing but whisky."

The old Highland woman who had charge of the odd little cottage in which Lavender lived was put into a state of violent consternation by

the arrival of these two strangers ; but as
Lavender said he would sleep on a couple of
chairs, and give his bed to Mosenberg, and the
sofa to Eyre, and as Mosenberg declared that the
house was a marvel of neatness and comfort, and
as Johnny assured her that he had frequently
slept in a herring-barrel, she grew gradually
pacified.   There was little difficulty about plates
and knives and forks at luncheon, which con-
sisted of cold mutton and two bottles of ale that
had somehow been overlooked ; but all these
minor inconveniences were soon smoothed over ;
and then Lavender, carrying his canvas under
his arm, and a portable easel over his shoulder,
went down to the shore, bade his companions
good-bye for a couple of hours, and left them
to explore the winding and rocky coast of
Jura.

In the evening they had dinner in a small
parlour, which was pretty well filled with a
chest of drawers, a sofa, and a series of large
canvasses.   There was a peat-fire burning in the
grate, and two candles on the table ; but the
small room did not get oppressively hot, for each
time the door was opened a draught of cold
sea-air rushed in from the passage, sometimes
blowing out one of the candles, but always
sweetening the atmosphere.   Then Johnny had

some fine tobacco with him; and Mosenberg
had brought Lavender a present of a meer-
schaum pipe; and presently a small kettle of
hot water was put in requisition, and the friends
drew round the fire.

"Well, it *is* good of you to come and see a
fellow like this," Lavender said, with a very
apparent and hearty gratitude in his face; "I
can scarcely believe my eyes that it is true.
And can you make any stay, Johnny? Have
you brought your colours with you?"

"Oh no, I don't mean to work," Johnny said.
"I have always had a fancy for a mid-winter cruise.
It's a hardening sort of thing, you know. You
soon get used to it, don't you, Mosenberg?"

And Johnny grinned.

"Not yet—I may afterwards," said the lad.
"But at present this is more comfortable than
being on deck at night when it rains and you
know not where you are going."

"But that was only your own perversity.
You might just as well have stopped in the
cabin and played that cornopean, and made
yourself warm and comfortable. Really, Lavender, it's very good fun; and if you only
watch for decent weather, you can go anywhere.
Fancy our coming round the Mull with the
Phœbe yesterday! And we had quite a pleasant
trip across to Islay."

"And where do you propose to go after leaving Jura?" Lavender asked.

"Well, you know, the main object of our cruise was to come and see you. But if you care to come with us for a few days, we will go wherever you like."

"If you are going further north, I must go with you," Lavender said, "for you are bound to drown yourself some day, Johnny, if some one doesn't take care of you."

There was no deep design in this project of Johnny's; but he had had a vague impression that Lavender might like to go north, if only to have a passing glimpse at the island he used to know.

"One of my fellows is well acquainted with the Hebrides," he said; "if you don't think it too much of a risk, I should like it myself; for those northern islands must look uncommonly wild and savage in winter; and one likes to have new experiences. Fancy, Mosenberg, what material you will get for your next piece— it will be full of storms, and seas, and thunder ——you know how the wind whistles through the overture to the *Diamants de la Couronne*——"

"It will whistle through us," said the boy, with an anticipatory shiver; "but I do not mind the wind if it is not wet. It is the wet that makes a boat so disagreeable—everything is so cold and clammy—you can touch nothing, and when you put your head up in the morning—pah! a dash of rain and mist, and salt water altogether gives you a shock——"

"What made you come round the Mull, Johnny, instead of cutting through the Crinan?" Lavender asked of his friend.

"Well," said the youth, modestly, "nothing except that two or three men said we couldn't do it."

"I thought so," Lavender said. "And I see I must go with you, Johnny. You must play no more of these tricks. You must watch your time, and run her quietly up the Sound of Jura to Crinan; and watch again and get her up to Oban; and watch again and get her up to Loch Sligachan. Then you may consider. It is quite possible you may have fine, clear weather if there is a moderate north-east wind blowing——"

"A north-east wind!" Mosenberg cried.

"Yes," Lavender replied, confidently, for he had not forgotten what Sheila used to teach him; "that is your only chance. If you have been living in fog for a fortnight, you will never forget your gratitude to a north-easter when it suddenly sets in to lift the clouds and show you a bit of blue sky. But it may knock us about a bit in crossing the Minch."

" We have come round the Mull, and we can go anywhere," Johnny said. " I'd back the *Phœbe* to take you safely to the West Indies ; wouldn't you, Mosenberg ? "

" Oh no," the boy said. " I would back her to take you, not to take me."

Two or three days thereafter the *Phœbe* was brought up the Sound from Port Ellen, and such things as were meant as a present to Lavender were landed. Then the three friends embarked ; for the weather had cleared considerably, and there was, indeed, when they set out, a pale, wintry sunshine gleaming on the sea, and on the white deck and spars of the handsome little cutter which Johnny commanded. The *Phœbe* was certainly a great improvement on the crank craft in which he used to adventure his life on Loch Fyne : she was big enough, indeed, to give plenty of work to everybody on board of her, and when once she had got into harbour, and things put to rights, her chief state-room proved a jolly and comfortable little place enough. They had some pleasant evenings in this way after the work of the day was over ; when the swinging lamps shone down on the table that was furnished with wine-glasses, bottles, cigars, and cards. Johnny was very proud of being in command, and of his exploit in doubling the Mull. He was continually consulting charts and compasses, and going on deck to communicate his last opinion to his skipper. Mosenberg, too, was getting better accustomed to the hardships of yatching, and learning how to secure a fair amount of comfort. Lavender never said that he wished to go near Lewis; but there was a sort of tacit understanding that their voyage should tend in that direction.

They had a little rough weather on reaching Skye, and, in consequence, remained in harbour a couple of days. At the end of that time a happy opportunity presented itself of cutting across the Little Minch—the Great Minch was considered a trifle risky—to Loch Maddy in North Uist. They were now in the Western Islands; and strange indeed was the appearance which the bleak region presented at this time of the year—the lonely coasts, the multitudes of wild fowl, the half-savage, wondering inhabitants, the treeless wastes, and desolate rocks. What these remote and melancholy islands might have looked like in fog and misty rain could only be imagined, however; for fortunately, the longed-for north-easter had set in, and there were wan glimmerings of sunshine across the sea and the solitary shores. They remained in Loch Maddy but a single day; and then, still favoured by a brisk north-east breeze, made their way through the Sound of Harris, and got to leeward of the conjoint island of Harris and Lewis. There, indeed, were the great mountains which Lavender had seen many a time from the north; and now they were close at hand, and dark, and forbidding. The days were brief at this time, and they were glad to put into Loch Resort, which Lavender had once seen in company with old Mackenzie, when they had come into the neighbourhood on a salmon-fishing excursion.

The *Phœbe* was at her anchorage, the clatter on deck over, and Johnny came below to see what sort of repast could be got for the evening. It was not a very grand meal, but he said—

" I propose that we have a bottle of champagne to celebrate our arrival at the island of Lewis. Did you ever see anything more successfully done? And now, if this wind continues, we can creep up to-morrow to Loch Roag, Lavender, if you would like to have a look at it."

For a moment the colour forsook Lavender's face.

" No, thank you, Johnny," he was about to say, when his friend interrupted him.

"Look here, Lavender; I know you would like to see the place, and you can do it easily without being seen. No one knows me. When we anchor in the bay, I suppose Mr. Mackenzie —as is the hospitable and praiseworthy custom of these parts—will send a message to the yacht and ask us to dine with him. I, at any rate, can go up and call on him, and make excuses for you ; and then I could tell you, you know——"

Johnny hesitated.

"Would you do that for me, Johnny ? " Lavender said. "Well, you are a good fellow."

"Oh," Johnny said, lightly, "it's a capital adventure for me ; and perhaps I could ask Mackenzie—Mr. Mackenzie, I beg your pardon —to let me have two or three clay pipes, for this brier root is rapidly going to the devil."

"He will give you anything he has in the house ; you never saw such a hospitable fellow, Johnny. But you must take great care what you do."

"You trust to me. In the meantime, let's see what Pate knows about Loch Roag."

Johnny called down his skipper, a bluff, short, red-faced man, who presently appeared, his cap in his hand.

"Will you have a glass of champagne, Pate ? "

"Oh, ay, sir," he said, not very eagerly.

"Would you rather have a glass of whisky?"

"Well, sir," Pate said, in accents that showed that his Highland pronunciation had been corrupted by many years' residence in Greenock, "I was thinkin' the whisky was a wee thing better for ye on a cauld nicht."

"Here you are, then. Now, tell me, do you know Loch Roag?"

"Oh, ay, fine. Many's the time I hiv been in to Borvabost."

"But," said Lavender, "do you know the Loch itself? Do you know the bay on which Mackenzie's house stands?"

"Weel, I'm no sae sure about that, sir. But if ye want to gang there, we can pick up some bit body at Borvabost that will tak' us round."

"Well," Lavender said, "I think I can tell you how to go. I know the channel is quite simple—there are no rocks about—and once you are round the point you will see your anchorage."

"It's twa or three years since I was there, sir," Pate remarked, as he put the glass back on the table; "I mind there was a daft auld man there that played the pipes."

"That was old John the Piper!" Lavender said. "Don't you remember Mr. Mackenzie, whom they call the King of Borva?"

" Weel, sir, I never saw him, but I was aware
he was in the place.   I have never been up here
afore wi' a party o' gentlemen, and he wasna
coming down to see the like o' us."

With what a strange feeling Lavender beheld,
the following afternoon, the opening to the great
Loch that he knew so well.   He recognized the
various rocky promontories, the Gaelic names of
which Sheila had translated for him.   Down
there in the south were the great heights of
Suainabhal, and Cracabhal, and Mealasabhal.
Right in front was the sweep of Borvabost Bay,
and its huts, and its small garden patches ; and
up beyond it was the hill on which Sheila used
to sit in the evening, to watch the sun go down
behind the Atlantic.   It was like entering again
a world with which he had once been familiar,
and in which he had left behind a peaceful
happiness he had sought in vain elsewhere.
Somehow, as the yacht dipped to the waves, and
slowly made her way into the loch, it seemed to
him that he was coming home—that he was
returning to the old and quiet joys he had
experienced there—that all the past time that
had darkened his life was now to be removed.
But when, at last, he saw Mackenzie's house
high up there over the tiny bay, a strange thril
of excitement passed through him, and that was

followed by a cold feeling of despair, which he did not seek to remove.

He stood on the companion, his head only being visible, and directed Pate until the *Phœbe* had arrived at her moorings; and then he went below. He had looked wistfully for a time up to the square, dark house, with its scarlet copings, in the vague hope of seeing some figure he knew; but now, sick at·heart, and fearing that Mackenzie might make him out with a glass, he sat down in the state-room, alone, and silent, and miserable.

He was startled by the sound of oars, and got up and listened. Mosenberg came down and said—

"Mr. Mackenzie has sent a tall, thin man—do you know him?—to see who we are, and whether we will go up to his house."

"What did Eyre say?"

"I don't know. I suppose he is going."

Then Johnny himself came below. He was a sensitive young fellow; and at this moment he was very confused, excited, and nervous.

"Lavender," he said, stammering somewhat, "I am going up now to Mackenzie's house. You know whom I shall see. Shall I take any message—if I see a chance—if your name is mentioned—a hint, you know——"

"Tell her," Lavender said, with a sudden pallor of determination in his face : but he stopped, and said abruptly, "Never mind, Johnny. Don't say anything about me."

"Not to-night, anyway," Johnny said to himself, as he drew on his best blue jacket, with its shining brass buttons, and went up the companion to see if the small boat was ready.

Johnny had had a good deal of knocking about the Western Highlands, and was familiar with the frank and ready hospitality which the local lairds—more particularly in the remote islands, where a stranger brought recent newspapers and a breath of the outer world with him—granted to all comers who bore with them the credentials of owning a yacht. But never before had he gone up to a strange house with such perturbation of spirit. He had been so anxious, too, that he had left no time for preparation. When he started up the hill, he could see, in the gathering dusk, that the tall keeper had just entered the house, and when he arrived there, he found absolutely nobody about the place.

In ordinary circumstances he would simply have walked in, and called some one from the kitchen. But he now felt himself somewhat of a spy ; and was not a little afraid of meeting the handsome Mrs. Lavender, of whom he had heard so much. There was no light in the passage; but there was a bright-red gloom in one of the windows, and, almost inadvertently, he glanced in there. What was this strange picture he saw? The red flame of the fire showed him the grand figures on the walls of Sheila's dining-room, and lit up the white table-cover and the crystal in the middle of the apartment. A beautiful young girl, clad in a tight blue dress, had just risen from beside the fire to light two candles that were on the table; and then she went back to her seat, and took up her sewing, but not to sew. For Johnny saw her gently kneel down beside a little bassinet that was a mass of wonderful pink and white, and he supposed the door in the passage was open, for he could hear a low voice humming some lullaby-song, sung by the young mother to her child. He went back a step, bewildered by what he had seen. Could he fly down to the shore, and bring Lavender up to look at this picture through the window, and beg of him to go in and throw himself on her forgiveness and mercy? He had not time to think twice. At this moment Mairi appeared in the dusky passage, looking a little scared, although she did not drop the plates she carried.

"Oh, sir, and are you the gentleman that has

come in the yacht?　And, Mr. Mackenzie, he is
upstairs just now, but he will be down ferry
soon ; and will you come in and speak to Miss
Sheila ? "

" *Miss Sheila ?* " he repeated to himself, with
amazement ; and the next moment he found
himself before this beautiful young girl, apologiz-
ing to her, stammering, and wishing that he had
never undertaken such a task, while he knew
that all the time she was regarding him with her
large, calm, and gentle eyes, and that there was
no trace of embarrassment in her manner.

" Will you take a seat by the fire until papa
comes down ? " she said.　" We are very glad to
have anyone come to see us ; we do not have
many visitors in the winter."

" But I am afraid," he stammered, " I am
putting you to trouble——" and he glanced at
the swinging pink and white couch.

" Oh no," Sheila said, with a smile, " I was
just about to send my little boy to bed."

She lifted the sleeping child and rolled it in
some enormous covering of white and silken-
haired fur, and gave the small bundle to Mairi
to carry to Scarlett.

" Stop a bit ? " Johnny called out to Mairi ;
and the girl started and looked round, whereupon he said to Sheila, with much blushing,

"Isn't there a superstition about an infant waking to find silver in its hand? I am sure you wouldn't mind my——"

"He cannot hold anything yet," Sheila said, with a smile.

"Then, Mairi, you must put this below his pillow—is not that the same thing for luck?" he said, addressing the young Highland girl as if he had known her all his life; and Mairi went away proud and pleased to have this precious bundle to carry, and talking to it with a thousand soft and endearing phrases in her native tongue.

Mackenzie came in, and found the two talking together.

"How do you do, sir?" he said, with a grave courtesy. "You are ferry welcome to the island, and if there is anything you want for the boat, you will hef it from us. She is a little thing to hef come so far."

"She's not very big," Johnny said, "but she's a thorough good sailor; and then we watch our time, you know. But I don't think we shall go further north than Lewis."

"Hef you no friends on board with you?" Mackenzie asked.

"Oh yes," Johnny answered; "two. But we did not wish to invade your house in a body. To-morrow——"

"To-morrow!" said Mackenzie, impatiently. "No, but to-night! Duncan, come here! Duncan, go down to the boat that has just come in and tell the gentlemen——"

"I beg your pardon, sir," Johnny cried, "but my two friends are regularly done up—tired— they were just going to turn in when I left the yacht. To-morrow, now, you will see them——"

"Oh, ferry well, ferry well," said Mackenzie, who had hoped to have a big dinner-party for Sheila's amusement. "In any way, you will stop and hef some dinner? It is just ready— oh, yes—and it is not a ferry fine dinner; but it will be different from your cabin for you to sit ashore."

"Well, if you will excuse me," Johnny was about to say, for he was so full of the news that he had to tell that he would have sacrificed twenty dinners to have got off at this moment. But Mr. Mackenzie would take no denial. An additional cover was laid for the stranger, and Johnny sat down to stare at Sheila in a furtive way, and to talk to her father about everything that was happening in the great world.

"And what now is this," said Mackenzie, with a lofty and careless air, "what is this I see in the capers about pictures painted by a gentleman called Lavender? I hev a great interest in these exhibitions: perhaps you hev seen the pictures?"

Johnny blushed very red; but he hid his face over his plate; and presently he answered, without daring to look at Sheila—

"I should think I have seen them! Why, if you care for coast landscapes, I can tell you you never saw such thorough good work all your life! Why, everybody's talking of them—you never heard of a man making such a name for himself in so short a time."

He ventured to look up. There was a strange, proud light in the girl's face; and the effect of it on this bearer of good tidings was to make him launch into such praises of these pictures as considerably astonished old Mackenzie. As for Sheila, she was proud and happy, but not surprised. She had known it all along. She had waited for it patiently, and it had come at last, although she was not to share in his triumph.

"I know some people who know him," said Johnny, who had taken two or three glasses of Mackenzie's sherry, and felt bold; "and what a shame it is he should go away from all his friends and almost cease to have any communication with them. And then, of all the

places in the world to spend a winter in, Jura
is about the very——"

"Jura!" said Sheila, quickly, and he fancied
that her face paled somewhat.

"I believe so," he said; "somewhere on
the western coast, you know, over the Sound
of Islay."

Sheila was obviously very much agitated;
but her father said in a careless way, "Oh yes,
Jura is not a ferry good place in the winter.
And the west side you said? Ay, there are
not many houses on the west side; it is not
a ferry good place to live in. But it will be
ferry cheap, whatever."

"I don't think that is the reason of his living
there," said Johnny, with a laugh.

"But," Mackenzie urged, rather anxiously,
"you wass not saying he would get much for
these pictures? Oh no, who will give much
money for pictures of rocks and seaweed?
Oh no!"

"Oh, won't they, though?" Johnny cried.
"They give a good deal more for that sort of
picture now than for the old-fashioned cottage-
scenes, with a young lady, dressed in a drugget
petticoat and a pink jacket, sitting peeling potatoes. Don't you make any mistake about that.
The public is beginning to learn what real good

work is, and, by Jove, don't they pay for it, too? Lavender got 800*l.* for the smaller of the two pictures I told you about."

Johnny was beginning to forget that the knowledge he was showing of Frank Lavender's affairs was suspiciously minute.

"Oh no, sir," Mackenzie said, with a frown. "It is all nonsense the stories that you hear. I hef had great experience of these exhibitions. I hef been to London several times, and every time I wass in the Exhibitions."

"But I should know something of it, too; for I am an artist myself."

"And do you get 800*l.* for a small picture?" Mackenzie asked, severely.

"Well, no," Johnny said, with a laugh. "But then I am a duffer."

After dinner, Sheila left the room; Johnny fancied he knew where she was going. He pulled in a chair to the fire, lit his pipe, and said he would have but one glass of toddy, which Mackenzie proceeded to make for him. And then he said to the old King of Borva—

"I beg your pardon, sir; but will you allow me to suggest that that young girl who was in here before dinner should not call your daughter Miss Sheila before strangers?"

"Oh, it is very foolish!" said Mackenzie,

"but it is an old habit, and they will not stop it. And Duncan, he is worse than anyone."

"Duncan, I suppose, is the tall fellow who waited at dinner?"

"Oh aye, that is Duncan."

Johnny's ingenious bit of stratagem had failed. He wanted to have old Mackenzie call his daughter Mrs. Lavender, so that he might have had occasion to open the question and plead for his friend. But the old man resolutely ignored the relationship between Lavender and his daughter, so far as this stranger was concerned; and so Johnny had to go away partly disappointed.

But another opportunity might occur; and in the meantime was not he carrying rare news down to the *Phœbe?* He had lingered too long in the house; but now he made up for lost time, and once or twice nearly missed his footing in running down the steep path. He had to find the small boat for himself, and go out on the slippery stones and seaweed to get into her. Then he pulled away from the shore, his oars striking white fire into the dark water, the water gurgling at the bow. Then he got into the shadow of the black hull of the yacht, and Pate was there to lower the little gangway.

R 2

When Johnny stepped on deck, he paused, in considerable doubt as to what he should do. He wished to have a word with Lavender alone; how could he go down with such a message as he had to deliver to a couple of fellows probably smoking and playing chess?

"Pate," he said, "tell Mr. Lavender I want him to come on deck for a minute."

" He's by himsel', sir," Pate said. " He's been sitting by himsel' for the last hour. The young gentleman's lain doon."

Johnny went down into the little cabin; Lavender, who had neither book, nor cigar, nor any other sign of occupation near him, seemed in his painful anxiety almost incapable of asking the question that rose to his lips.

" Have you seen her, Johnny?" he said, at length, with his face looking strangely careworn.

Johnny was an impressionable young fellow. There were tears running freely down his cheeks, as he said—

" Yes, I have, Lavender; and she was rocking a child in a cradle."

CHAPTER VIII.

REDINTEGRATIO AMORIS.

THAT same night Sheila dreamed a strange dream ; and it seemed to her that an angel of God came to her, and stood before her, and looked at her with his shining face and his sad eyes. And he said, "*Are you a woman, and yet slow to forgive? Are you a mother, and have you no love for the father of your child?*" It seemed to her that she could not answer. She fell on her knees before him, and covered her face with her hands, and wept. And when she raised her eyes again, the angel was gone ; and in his place Ingram was there, stretching out his hand to her, and bidding her rise and be comforted. Yet he, too, spoke in the same reproachful tones, and said—

"What would become of us all, Sheila, if none of our actions were to be condoned by time and repentance? What would become of us if we could not say, at some particular point of our lives, to the bygone time, that we had left it, with all its errors, and blunders, and follies, behind us, and would, with the help of God, start clear on a new sort of life? What would it be if there were no forgetfulness for any of us—no kindly veil to come down and shut out the memory of what we have done—if the staring record were to be kept for ever before our eyes? And you are a woman, Sheila—it should be easy for you to forgive, and to encourage, and to hope for better things of the man you love. Has he not suffered enough? Have you no word for him?"

The sound of her sobbing in the night-time brought her father to the door. He tapped at the door, and said—

"What is the matter, Sheila?"

She awoke with a slight cry; and he went into the room and found her in a strangely troubled state, her hands outstretched to him, her eyes wet and wild.

"Papa, I have been very cruel. I am not fit to live any more. There is no woman in the world would have done what I have done."

"Sheila!" he said, "you hef been dreaming again about all that folly and nonsense. Lie down, like a good lass. You will wake the boy if you do not lie down and go to sleep ; and to-morrow we will pay a visit to the yacht that hass come in, and you will ask the gentlemen to look at the *Maighdean-mhara.*"

" Papa," she said, " to-morrow I want you to take me to Jura."

" To Jura, Sheila ? You cannot go to Jura! You cannot leave the baby with Mairi, Sheila."

" I will take him with me," she said.

" Oh, it is not possible at all, Sheila. But I will go to Jura. Oh yes, I will go to Jura. Indeed, I was thinking last night that I would go to Jura."

" Oh no, *you* must not go," she cried. " You would speak harshly—and he is very proud— and we should never see each other again. Papa, I know you will do this for me—you will let me go——"

" It is foolish of you, Sheila," her father said, " to think that I do not know how to arrange such a thing without making a quarrel of it. But you will see all about it in the morning. Just now, you will lie down, like a good lass, and go to sleep. So good night, Sheila, and do not think of it any more till the morning."

She thought of it all through the night, however. She thought of her sailing away down through the cold wintry seas to search that lonely

coast.   Would the grey dawn break with snow;
or would the kindly heavens lend her some fair
sunlight as she set forth on her lonely quest?
And all the night through she accused herself of
being hard of heart; and blamed herself,
indeed, for all that had happened in the bygone
time.   Just as the day was coming in she fell
asleep; and she dreamed that she went to the
angel whom she had seen before, and knelt down
at his feet, and repeated in some vague way the
promises she had made on her marriage morning.
With her head bent down, she said that she
would live and die a true wife, if only another
chance were given her.   The angel answered
nothing; but he smiled with his sad eyes, and
put his hand for a moment on her head, and
then disappeared.   When she woke Mairi was
in the room, silently stealing away the child;
and the white daylight was clear in the windows.

She dressed with trembling hands, and yet
there was a faint suffused sense of joy in her heart.
She wondered if her father would keep to his
promise of the night before, or whether it had
been made to get her to rest.   In any case, she
knew that he could not refuse her much; and
had not he himself said that he intended going
away down to Jura?

"Sheila, you are not looking well this morning," her father said ; "it is foolish of you to lie awake and think of such things. And as for what you wass saying about Jura, how can you go to Jura? We hef no boat big enough for that. I could go—oh yes, I could go—but the boat I would get at Stornoway you could not go in it at all, Sheila ; and as for the baby——"

"But then, Papa," she said, "did not the gentleman who was here last night say they were going back by Jura? And it is a big yatch ; and he has only two friends on board. He might take us down."

"You cannot ask a stranger, Sheila. Besides, the boat is too small a one for this time of the year. I should not like to see you go in her, Sheila."

"I have no fear," the girl said.

"No fear!" her father said, impatiently. "No, of course you hef no fear—that is the mischief. You will tek no care of yourself whatever."

"When is the young gentleman coming up this morning?"

"Oh, he will not come up again till I go down. Will you go down to the boats, Sheila, and go on board of her?"

Sheila assented ; and some half hour there-after she stood at the door, clad in her tight-fitting blue serge, with the hat and sea-gull's wing over her splendid masses of hair. It was an angry-looking morning enough; rags of grey cloud were being hurried past the shoulders of Suainabhal; a heavy surf was beating on the shore.

"There is going to be rain, Sheila," her father said, smelling the moisture in the keen air. "Will you hef your waterproof?"

"Oh no," she said; "if I am to meet strangers, I cannot wear a waterproof."

The sharp wind had brought back the colour to her cheeks; and there was some gladness in her eyes. She knew she might have a fight for it, before she could persuade her father to set sail in this strange boat; but she never doubted for a moment—recollecting the gentle face and modest manner of the youthful owner—that he would be really glad to do her a service, and she knew that her father's opposition would give way.

"Shall we take Bras, papa?"

"No, no!" her father said; "we will hef to go in a small boat. I hope you will not get wet, Sheila—there is a good breeze on the water this morning."

"I think they are much safer in here than going round the islands just at present," Sheila said.

"Ay, you are right there, Sheila," her father said, looking at the direction of the wind. "They got in in ferry good time. And they may hef to stay here for a while before they can face the sea again."

"And we shall become very great friends with them, Papa; and they will be glad to take us to Jura," she said, with a smile; for she knew there was not much of the hospitality of Borvabost bestowed with ulterior motives.

They went down the steep path to the bay, where the *Phœbe* was lurching and heaving in the rough swell, her bowsprit sometimes nearly catching the crest of a wave. No one was on deck. How were they to get on board?

"They can't hear you in this wind," Sheila said. "We will have to haul down our own boat."

And that, indeed, they had to do; though the work of getting the little thing down the beach was not very arduous for a man of Mackenzie's build.

"I am going to pull you out to the yacht, papa," Sheila said.

"Indeed you will do no such thing," her father said, indignantly. "As if you wass a fisherman's lass, and the gentlemen never wass seeing you before. Sit down in the stern, Sheila, and hold on ferry tight, for it is a rough water for this little boat."

They had almost got out indeed to the yacht before anyone was aware of their approach; but Pate appeared in time to seize the rope that Mackenzie flung him, and, with a little scrambling, they were at last safely on board. The noise of their arrival, however, startled Johnny Eyre, who was lying on his back smoking a pipe after breakfast. He jumped up, and said to Mosenberg, who was his only companion—

"Hillo! here's this old gentleman come on board. He knows you? What's to be done?"

"Done?" said the boy, with a moment's hesitation; and then a flush of decision sprang into his face. "Ask him to come down. Yes; I will speak to him, and tell him that Lavender is on the island. Perhaps he meant to go into the house; who knows? If he did not, let us make him!"

"All right," said Johnny; "let's go a buster."

Then he called up the companion to Pate, to send the gentleman below, while he flung a few things aside, to make the place more presentable, Johnny had been engaged, a few minutes before, in sewing a button on a woollen shirt; and that article of attire does not look well beside a breakfast-table.

His visitor began to descend the narrow wooden steps; and presently Mackenzie was heard to say—

"'Tek great care, Sheila. The brass is ferry slippery."

"Oh, thunder!" Johnny said, looking to Mosenberg.

"Good morning, Mr. Eyre," said the old King of Borva, stooping to get into the cabin; "it is a rough day you are getting. Sheila, mind your head till you have passed the door."

Mackenzie came forward to shake hands, and in doing so caught sight of Mosenberg. The whole truth flashed upon him in a moment; and he instantaneously turned to Sheila, and said, quickly—

"Sheila, go up on deck for a moment."

But she, too, had seen the lad; and she came forward, with a pale face, but with a perfectly self-possessed manner, and said, "How do you do? It is a surprise, your coming to the island; but you often used to talk of it."

"Yes," he stammered, as he shook hands with her and her father, "I often wished to come here. What a wild place it is! And have you lived here, Mrs. Lavender, all the time since you left London ? "

" Yes, I have."

Mackenzie was getting very uneasy. Every moment he expected Lavender would enter this confined little cabin ; and was this the place for these two to meet, before a lot of acquaintances ?

" Sheila," he said, " it is too close for you here, and I am going to have a pipe with the gentlemen. Now if you wass a good lass, you would go ashore again, and go up to the house, and say to Mairi that we will all come for luncheon at one o'clock, and she must get some fish up from Borvabost. Mr. Eyre, he will send a man ashore with you in his own boat, that is bigger than mine, and you will show him the creek to put into. Now go away, like a good lass, and we will be up ferry soon—oh yes, we will be up directly at the house."

" I am sure," Sheila said to Johnny Eyre, " we can make you more comfortable up at the house than you are here, although it is a nice little cabin." And then she turned to Mosenberg, and said, " And we have a great many things to talk about."

" Could she suspect ? " Johnny asked himself, as he escorted her to the boat, and pulled her in himself to the shore. Her face was pale, and her manner a trifle formal; otherwise she showed no sign. He watched her go along the stones till she reached the path; then he pulled out to the *Phœbe* again, and went down below to entertain his host of the previous evening.

Sheila walked slowly up the rude little path, taking little heed of the blustering wind and the hurrying clouds. Her eyes were bent down; her face was pale. When she got to the top of the hill, she looked, in a blank sort of way, all round the bleak moorland; but probably she did not expect to see anyone there. Then she walked, with rather an uncertain step, into the house.

She looked into the room, the door of which stood open. Her husband sate there, with his arms outstretched on the table, and his head buried in his hands. He did not hear her approach, her footfall was so light; and it was with the same silent step she went into the room, and knelt down beside him, and put her hands and face on his knee, and said simply—

"I beg for your forgiveness."

He started up and looked at her as though she were some spirit, and his own face was haggard and strange.

"Sheila," he said, in a low voice, laying his

hand gently on her head, "it is I who ought to be there, and you know it. But I cannot meet your eyes. I am not going to ask for your forgiveness just yet—I have no right to expect it. All I want is this—if you will let me come and see you just as before we were married— and if you will give me a chance of winning your consent over again—we can at least be friends until then—— But why do you cry, Sheila? You have nothing to reproach yourself with."

She rose, and regarded him for a moment with her streaming eyes; and then, moved by the passionate entreaty of her face, and forgetting altogether the separation and time of trial he had proposed, he caught her to his bosom, and kissed her forehead, and talked soothingly and caressingly to her, as if she were a child.

"I cry," she said, "because I am happy— because I believe all that time is over—because I think you will be kind to me. And I will try to be a good wife to you; and you will forgive me all that I have done."

"You are heaping coals of fire on my head, Sheila," he said, humbly. "You know I have nothing to forgive. As for you—I tell you I have no right to expect your forgiveness yet. But I think you will find out by and by that my repentance is not a mere momentary thing. I have had a long time to think over what has happened—and what I lost when I lost you, Sheila."

"But you have found me again," the girl said, pale a little, and glad to sit down on the nearest couch, while she held his hand and drew him towards her. "And now I must ask you for one thing."

He was sitting beside her : he feared no longer to meet the look of those earnest, meek, affectionate eyes.

"This is it," she said. "If we are to be together, not what we were, but something quite different from that, will you promise me never to say one word about what is past—to shut it out altogether—to forget it ? "

"I cannot, Sheila," he said. "Am I to have no chance of telling you how well I know how cruel I was to you—how sorry I am for it ? "

"No," she said, firmly. "If you have some things to regret, so have I ; and what is the use of competing with each other as to which has the most forgiveness to ask for ? Frank, dear, you will do this for me. You will promise never to speak one word about that time."

How earnest the beautiful, sad face was ! He could not withstand the entreaty of the piteous eyes.   He said to her, abashed by the great love that she showed, and hopeless of making other reparation than obedience to her generous wish—

"Let it be so, Sheila.   I will never speak a word about it.   You will see otherwise than in words whether I forget what is passed, and your goodness in letting it go.   But, Sheila," he added, with downcast face, "Johnny Eyre was here last night—he told me——" He had to say no more.   She took his hand, and led him gently and silently out of the room.

Meanwhile the old King of Borva had been spending a somewhat anxious time down in the cabin of the *Phœbe*.   Many and many a day had he been planning a method by which he might secure a meeting between Sheila and her husband; and now it had all come about without his aid, and in a manner which rendered him unable to take any precautions.   He did not know but that some awkward accident might destroy all the chances of the affair.   He knew that Lavender was in the island.   He had frankly asked young Mosenberg as soon as Sheila had left the yacht.

"Oh yes," the lad said, "he went away into the island early this morning.   I begged of him to go to your house; he did not answer. But I am sure he will. I know he will."

"My Kott!" Mackenzie said, "and he has been wandering about the island all the morning, and he will be very faint and hungry; and a man is neffer in a good temper then for making up a quarrel. If I had known the last night, I could hef had dinner with you all here, and we should hef given him a good glass of whisky, and then it wass a good time to tek him up to the house."

"Oh, you may depend on it, Mr. Mackenzie," Johnny Eyre said, "that Lavender needs no stimulus of that sort to make him desire a reconciliation. No, I should think not. He has done nothing but brood over this affair ever since he left London; and I should not be surprised if you scarcely knew him, he is so altered. You would fancy he had lived ten years in the time."

"Ay, ay," Mackenzie said, not listening very attentively, and evidently thinking more of what might be happening elsewhere; "but I was thinking, gentlemen, it wass time for us to go ashore, and go up to the house, and hef something to eat."

"I thought you said one o'clock for luncheon, sir," young Mosenberg said.

"One o'clock!" Mackenzie repeated, impatiently; "who the teffle can wait till one o'clock, if you hef been walking about an island since the daylight with nothing to eat or drink."

Mr. Mackenzie forgot that it was not Lavender he had asked to lunch.

"Oh yes," he said, "Sheila hass had plenty of time to send down to Borvabost for some fish; and by the time you get up to the house, you will see that it is ready."

"Very well," Johnny said, "we can go up to the house, any way."

He went up the companion, and he had scarcely got his head above the level of the bulwarks when he called back——

"I say, Mr. Mackenzie, here is Lavender on the shore, and your daughter is with him. Do they want to come on board do you think? Or do they want us to go ashore?"

Mackenzie uttered a few phrases in Gaelic, and got up on deck instantly. There, sure enough, was Sheila, with her hand on her husband's arm; and they were both looking towards the yacht. The wind was blowing too strong for them to call. Mackenzie wanted himself to pull in for them; but this was overruled; and Pate was despatched.

An awkward pause ensued. The three standing on deck were sorely perplexed as to the forthcoming interview, and as to what they should do. Were they to rejoice over a reconciliation; or ignore the fact altogether, and simply treat Sheila as Mrs. Lavender? Her father, indeed, fearing that Sheila would be strangely excited, and would probably burst into tears, wondered what he could get to scold her about.

Fortunately, an incident, partly ludicrous, broke the awkwardness of their arrival. The getting on deck was a matter of some little difficulty; in the scuffle Sheila's small hat with its snow-white feather got unloosed somehow, and the next minute it was whirled away by the wind into the sea. Pate could not be sent after it just at the moment, and it was rapidly drifting away to leeward, when Johnny Eyre, with a laugh and a "Here goes!" plunged in after the white feather that was dripping and rising in the waves like a sea-gull. Sheila uttered a slight cry, and caught her husband's arm. But there was not much danger. Johnny was an expert swimmer; and in a few minutes he was seen to be making his way backward with one arm, while in the other hand he held Sheila's hat. Then Pate had by this time got the small boat round to leeward; and very shortly after Johnny, dripping like a Newfoundland dog, came on deck and presented the hat to Sheila, amidst a vast deal of laughter.

"I am so sorry," she said; "but you must change your clothes quickly—I hope you will have no harm from it."

"Not I," he said, "but my beautiful white decks have got rather into a mess. I am glad you saw them while they were dry, Mrs. Lavender. Now I am going below to make myself a swell, for we're all going to have luncheon on shore, ain't we?"

Johnny went below very well pleased with himself. He had called her Mrs. Lavender without wincing. He had got over all the awkwardness of a second introduction by the happy notion of plunging after the hat. He had to confess, however, that the temperature of the sea was not just what he could have preferred for a morning bath.

By and by he made his appearance in his best suit of blue and brass buttons, and asked Mrs. Lavender if she would now come down and see the cabin.

"I think you want a good glass of whisky," old Mackenzie said, as they all went below, "the water it is ferry cold just now."

"Yes," Johnny said, blushing, "we shall all celebrate the capture of the hat."

It was the capture of the hat, then, that was to be celebrated by this friendly ceremony. Perhaps it was ; but there was no mirth now on Sheila's face.

"And you will drink first, Sheila," her father said, almost solemnly, "and you will drink to your husband's health."

Sheila took the glass of raw whisky in her hand ; and looked round timidly.

"I cannot drink this, papa," she said. "If you will let me——"

"You will drink that glass to your husband's health, Sheila," old Mackenzie said, with unusual severity.

"She shall do nothing of the sort if she doesn't like it ! " Johnny Eyre cried, suddenly— not caring whether it was the wrath of old Mackenzie or of the devil that he was braving ; and forthwith he took the glass out of Sheila's hand, and threw the whisky on the floor. Then he pulled out a champagne bottle from a basket and said, "This is what Mrs. Lavender will drink."

Mackenzie looked staggered for a moment. He had never been so braved before. But he was not in a quarrelsome mood on such an occasion; so he burst into a loud laugh, and cried——

"Well, did ever any man see the like o' that? Good whisky—ferry good whisky—and flung on the floor as if it was water; and as if there wass no one in the boat that would hef drunk it. But no matter, Mr. Eyre, no matter; the lass will drink whatever you give her, for she's a good lass; and if we hef all to drink champagne that is no matter too; but there is a man or two up on deck that would not like to know the whisky was spoiled."

"Oh," Johnny said, "there is still a drop left for them. And this is what you must drink, Mrs. Lavender."

Lavender had sat down in a corner of the cabin, his eyes averted. When he heard Sheila's name mentioned he looked up, and she came forward to him. She said, in a simple way, "I drink this to you, my dear husband," and at the same moment the old King of Borva came forward and held out his hand, and said, "Yes; and by Kott, I drink to your health, too, with ferry good will."

Lavender started to his feet.

. "Wait a bit, Mr. Mackenzie. I have got something to say to you before you ought to shake my hand."

But Sheila interposed quickly. She put her hand on his arm, and looked into his face.

"You will keep your promise to me," she said ; and that was an end of the matter. The two men shook hands ; there was nothing said between them, then or again, of what was over and gone.

They had a pleasant enough luncheon together, up in that quaint room, with the Tyrolese pictures on the wall ; and Duncan for once respected old Mackenzie's threats as to what would happen if he called Sheila anything but Mrs. Lavender before these strangers. For some time Lavender sat almost silent ; and answered Sheila, who continuously talked to him, in little else than monosyllables. But he looked at her a great deal, sometimes in a wistful sort of way, as if he were trying to recall the various fancies her face used to produce in his imagination.

"Why do you look at me so ?" she said in an undertone.

"Because I have made a new friend," he said.

But when Mackenzie began to talk of the wonders of the island and the seas around it, and to beg the young yachtsmen to prolong their stay, Lavender joined with a will in that conversation, and added his entreaties.

" Then you are going to stay ? " Johnny Eyre said, looking up.

" Oh, yes," he answered, as if the alternative of going back with them had not presented itself to him.

" For one thing, I have got to look out for a place where I can build a house. That is what I mean to do with my savings just at present; and if you would come with me, Johnny, and have a prowl round the island, to find out some pretty little bay with a good anchorage in it— for you know I am going to steal that *Maighdean-mhara* from Mr. Mackenzie—then we can begin and make ourselves architects, and plan out the place that is to be. And then some day——"

Mackenzie had been sitting in mute astonishment; but he suddenly broke in upon his son-in-law.

" On this island ? No, by Kott, you will not do that. On this island ? And with all the people at Stornoway ? Hoots, no, that will neffer do; Sheila, she hass no one to speak to on this island as a young lass should hef; and you—what would you do yourself in the bad weather ? But there is Stornoway—oh yes, that is a fine big place, and many people you will get to know there, and you will hef the newspapers and the letters at once; and there will be always boats there, that you can go to Oban, to Greenock, to Glasgow—anywhere in the world—whenever you hef a mind to do that; and then when you go to London, as you will hef to go many times, there will be plenty there to look after your house when it is shut up, and keep the rain out, and the paint and the paper good, more as could be done on this island. Oh, this island!—how would you live on this island?"

The old King of Borva spoke quite impatiently and contemptuously of the place. You would have thought his life on this island was a species of penal servitude; and that he dwelt in his solitary house only to think with a vain longing of the glories and delights of Stornoway. Lavender knew well what prompted these scornful comments on Borva. The old man was afraid that the island would really be too dull for Sheila and her husband; and that, whereas the easy compromise of Stornoway might be practicable, to set up house in Borva might lead them to abandon the north altogether.

"From what I have heard of it from Mr. Lavender," Johnny said, with a laugh, "I don't think this island such a dreadful place; and I'm hanged if I have found it so, so far."

"But you will know nothing about it—nothing whateffer," said Mackenzie, petulantly. "You do not know the bad weather, when you cannot go down the Loch to Callernish ; and you might hef to go to London just then."

"Well, I suppose London could wait," Johnny said.

Mackenzie began to get angry with this young man.

"You hef not been to Stornoway," he said, severely.

"No, I haven't," Johnny replied, with much coolness, "and I don't hanker after it. I get plenty of town life in London ; and when I come up to the sea and the islands I'd rather pitch my tent with you, sir, than live in Stornoway."

"Oh, but you don't know, Johnny, how fine a place Stornoway is," Lavender said, hastily, for he saw the old man was beginning to get vexed. "Stornoway was a beautiful little town, and it is on the sea, too——"

"And it hass fine houses, and ferry many people, and ferry good society whatever," Mackenzie added, with some touch of indignation.

"But you see, this is how it stands, Mr. Mackenzie," Lavender put in, humbly. "We should have to go to London from time to time, and we should then get quite enough of city

life, and you might find an occasional trip with
us not a bad thing. But up here I should have
to look on my house as a sort of work-shop.
Now, with all respect to Stornoway, you must
admit that the coast about here is a little
more picturesque. Besides, there's another
thing. It would be rather more difficult at
Stornoway to take a rod or a gun out of a
morning. Then there would be callers, bothering you at your work. Then Sheila would have
far less liberty in going about by herself."

"Eighthly and tenthly, you've made up your
mind to have a house here," cried Johnny Eyre
with a loud laugh.

"Sheila says she would like to have a billiard-
room," her husband continued. "Where could
you get that in Stornoway?"

"And you must have a large room for a
piano, to sing in, and play in," the young Jew-
boy said, looking at Sheila.

"I should think a one-storeyed house, with a
large verandah, would be the best sort of thing,"
Lavender said, "both for the sun and the rain;
and then one could have one's easle outside, you
know. Suppose we all go for a walk round the
shore by-and-by; there is too much of a breeze
to take the *Phœbe* down the loch."

So the King of Borva was quietly overruled

and his dominions invaded in spite of himself. Sheila could not go out with the gentlemen just then; she was to follow in about an hour's time; meanwhile they buttoned their coats, pulled down their caps tight, and set out to face the grey skies and the wintry wind. Just as they were passing away from the house, Mackenzie, who was walking in front with Lavender, said, in a cautious sort of way——

"You will want a deal of money to build this house you wass speaking about—for it will hef to be all stone and iron, and ferry strong whatever, or else it will be a plague to you from the one year to the next with the rain getting in."

"Oh yes," Lavender said, "it will have to be done well once for all; and what with rooms big enough to paint in, and play billiards in, and also a bedroom or two for friends who may come to stay with us, it will be an expensive business. But I have been very lucky, Mr. Mackenzie. It isn't the money I have, but the commissions I am offered, that warrant me going in for this house. I'll tell you about all these things afterwards. In the meantime I shall have 2,400l., or thereabouts, in a couple of months."

"But you hef more than that now," Mackenzie said, gravely. "This is what I wass going to tell you. The money that your aunt left, that is yours, every penny of it—oh yes, every penny and every farthing of it is yours, sure enough. For it wass Mr. Ingram hass told me all about it; and the old lady, she wanted him to take care of the money for Sheila; but what was the good of the money to Sheila? My lass, she will hef plenty of money of her own; and I wanted to hef nothing to do with what Mr. Ingram said—but it wass all no use, and there iss the money now for you and for Sheila, every penny and every farthing of it."

Mackenzie ended by talking in an injured way, as if this business had seriously increased his troubles.

"But you know," Lavender said with amazement, "you know as well as I do that this money was definitely left to Ingram, and—you may believe me or not—I was precious glad of it when I heard it. Of course it would have been of more use to him if he had not been about to marry this American lady——"

"Oh, you hef heard that, then?" Mackenzie said.

"Mosenberg brought me the news. But are you quite sure about this affair? Don't you think this is merely a trick of Ingram's, to enable him to give the money to Sheila? That would be very like him. I know him of old."

"Well, I cannot help it if a man will tell lies," said Mackenzie. "But that is what he says is true. And he will not touch the money—indeed, he will hef plenty, as you say—but there it is for Sheila and you; and you will be able to build whatever house you like. And if you wass thinking of having a bigger boat than the *Maighdean-mhara*———" the old man suggested.

Lavender jumped at that notion directly.

"What if we could get a yacht big enough to cruise anywhere in the summer months?" he said. "We might bring a party of people all the way from the Thames to Loch Roag, and cast anchor opposite Sheila's house. Fancy Ingram and his wife coming up like that in the autumn: and I know you could go over to Sir James and get us some shooting."

Mackenzie laughed grimly.

"We will see, we will see about that. I think there will be no great difficulty about getting a deer or two for you; and as for the salmon, there will be one or two left in the White Water—oh yes, we will hef a little shooting and a little fishing for any of your friends. And as for the boat, it will be ferry difficult to get a good big boat for such a purpose, without you wass planning and building one yourself; and

that will be better, I think ; for the yachts now-
a-days they are all built for the racing, and you
will hef a boat fifty tons, sixty tons, seventy tons,
that hass no room in her below, but is nothing
but a big heap of canvas and·spars.   But if you
wass wanting a good, steady boat, with good
cabins below for the leddies, and a good saloon
that you could hef your dinner in all at once,
then you will maybe come down with me to
a shipbuilder I know in Glasgow—oh, he is
aferry good man—and we will see what can be
done.   There is a gentleman now in Dunoon—
and they say he is a ferry great artist too—and
he hass a schooner of sixty tons that I hef been
in myself, and it wass just like a steamer below
for the comfort of it.   And when the boat is
ready, I will get you ferry good sailors for her,
that will know every bit of the coast from Loch-
Indaal to the Butt of Lewis, and I will see that
they are ferry cheap for you, for I hef plenty of
work for them in the winter.   But I wass no
saying yet," the old man added, "that you were
right about coming to live in Borva. Stornoway
is a good place to live in ; and it is a fine
harbour for repairs, ¨f the boat was wanting
repairs——"

"If she were, couldn't we send her round to
Stornoway ? "

"But the people in Stornoway—it iss the people in Stornoway," said Mackenzie, who was not going to give in without a grumble.

Well, they did not fix on a site for the house that afternoon. Sheila did not make her appearance. Lavender kept continually turning and looking over the long undulations of rock and moorland; and at length he said—

"Look here, Johnny, would you mind going on by yourselves? I think I shall walk back to the house."

"What is keeping that foolish girl?" her father said, impatiently. "It is something about the dinner, now, as if any one wass particular about a dinner in an island like this, where you can expect nothing. But at Stornoway— oh yes, they hef many things there."

"But I want you to come and dine with us on board the *Phœbe* to-night, sir," Johnny said. "It will be rather a lark, mind you; we make up a tight fit in that cabin. I wonder if Mrs. Lavender would venture; do you think she would, sir?"

"Oh no, not this evening, any way," said her father, "for I know she will expect you all to be up at the house this evening; and what would be the use of tumbling about in the bay when you can be in a house. But it is ferry kind of you—oh yes, to-morrow night, then we will go down to the boat—but this night, I know Sheila will be ferry sorry if you do not come to the house."

" Well, let's go back now," Johnny said, "and if we've time, we might go down for our guns and have a try along the shore for an hour or so before the daylight goes. Fancy that chance at those wild duck ! "

" Oh, but that is nothing," Mackenzie said, " to-morrow you will come with me up to the loch, and there you will hef some shooting : and in many other places I will show you, you will hef plenty of shooting."

They had just got back to the house when they found Sheila coming out. She had, as her father supposed, been detained by her preparations for entertaining their guests ; but now she was free until dinner-time, and so the whole party went down to the shore to pay a visit to the *Phœbe*, and let Mackenzie have a look at the guns on board. Then they went up to the house, and found the tall and grim keeper with the baby in his arms, while Scarlett and Mairi were putting the finishing touches on the gleaming white table and its show of steel and crystal.

How strange it was to Sheila to sit at dinner

there, and listen to her husband talking of boating and fishing and what not as he used to sit
and talk in the olden time to her father, on the
summer evenings, on the high rocks over Borvabost. The interval between that time and this
seemed to go clean out of her mind. And yet
there must have been some interval, for he was
looking older, and sterner, and much rougher
about the face now, after being buffetted about
by wind and rain and sun during that long and
solitary stay in Jura. But it was very like the
old times when they went into the little drawing-
room, and when Mairi brought in the hot water,
and the whisky, the tobacco and the long pipes;
when the old King of Borva sate himself down
in his great chair by the table, and when
Lavender came to Sheila, and asked her if he
would get out her music, and open the piano for
her.

"Madame," young Mosenberg said to her,
"it is a long time since I heard one of your
strange Gaelic songs."

"Perhaps you never heard this one," Sheila
said, and she began to sing the plaintive "Farewell to Glenshalloch." Many a time, indeed, of
late had she sung its simple and pathetic air as
a sort of lullaby, perhaps because it was gentle,
monotonous, and melancholy, perhaps because

there were lines here and there that she liked.
Many a time had she sung—

Sleep sound, my sweet babe, there is nought to alarm thee,
The sons of the valley no power have to harm thee !
I'll sing thee to rest in the balloch untrodden,
With a coronach sad for the slain of Culloden.

But long before she had reached the end of it
her father's patience gave way, and he said—

"Sheila, we will hef no more of those teffles
of songs ! We will hef a good song ; and there
is more than one of the gentlemen can sing a
good song, and we do not wish to be always
crying over the sorrows of other people. Now
be a good lass, Sheila, and sing us a good
cheerful song."

And Sheila, with great good-nature, suddenly
struck a different key, and sang, with a spirit
that delighted the old man—

The standard on the braes o' Mar,
Is up and streaming rarely !
The gathering pipe on Lochnagar,
Is sounding lang and clearly !
The Highlandmen, from hill and glen,
In martial hue, with bonnets blue,
Wi' belted plaids, and burnished blades,
Are coming late and early !

"Now that is a better kind of song—that is
a teffle of a good song !" Mackenzie cried,

keeping time to the music with his right foot, as if he were a piper playing in front of his regiment. "Wass their anything like that in your country, Mr. Mosenberg?"

"I don't know, sir," said the lad, meekly; "but if you like I will sing you one or two of our soldiers' songs. They have plenty of fire in them, I think."

Certainly, Mackenzie had plenty of brilliant, and cheerful, and stirring music that evening, but that which pleased him most, doubtless, was to see—as all the world could see—the happiness of his good lass. Sheila, proud and glad, with a light on her face that had not been there for many a day, wanted to do everything at once to please and amuse her guests, and most of all to wait upon her husband; and Lavender was so abashed by her sweet service and her simple ways that he could show his gratitude only by some furtive and kindly touch of the hand as Sheila passed. It seemed to him she had never looked so beautiful; and never, indeed, since they left Stornoway together, had he heard her quiet low laugh so full of enjoyment. What had he done, he asked himself, to deserve her confidence; for it was the hope in her proud and gentle eyes that gave that radiant brightness to her face? He did not know. He could not answer. Perhaps the forgiveness she had so freely and frankly tendered, and the confidence she now so clearly showed in him sprang from no judgment or argument, but were only the natural fruit of an abounding and generous love. More than once that night he wished that Sheila could read the next half-dozen years as though in some prophetic scroll, that he might show her how he would endeavour to prove himself if not worthy—for he could scarcely hope that— at least conscious of her great and unselfish affection, and as grateful for it as a man could be.

They pushed their enjoyment to such a late hour of the night that when they discovered what time it was, Mackenzie would not allow one of them to venture out into the dark to find the path down to the yacht; and Duncan and Scarlett were forthwith called on to provide the belated guests with some more or less haphazard sleeping accommodation.

"Mr. Mackenzie," said Johnny, "I don't mind a bit if I sleep on the floor. I've just had the jolliest night I ever spent in my life. Mosenberg, you'll have to take the *Phœbe* back to Greenock by yourself. I shall never leave Borva any more."

"You will be sober in the morning, Mr. Eyre,"

young Mosenberg said; but the remark was unjust, for Johnny's enthusiasm had not been produced by the old King's whisky, potent as that was.

CHAPTER IX.

THE PRINCESS SHEILA.

"I should like," said Mrs. Edward Ingram, sitting down and contentedly folding her hands in her lap, "I should so much like, Edward, to have my own way for once—it would be so novel and so nice."

Her husband was busy with a whole lot of plans all stretched out before him, and with a pipe which he had some difficulty in keeping alight. He did not even turn round as he answered—

"You have your own way always. But you can't expect to have mine also, you know."

"Do you remember," she said, slowly, "anything your friend Sheila told you about your rudeness to people? I wish, Edward, you would leave those ragged children and their school-houses for three minutes. Do! I so much want to see some places when we go to Scotland; for who knows when we may be there again? I

have set my heart on the Braes of Yarrow.
And Loch Awe by moonlight.   And the Pass
of Glencoe——"

"My dear child," he said, at last turning
round in his chair, "how can we go to those
places?   Sheila says Oban on the fifteenth."

"But what Sheila says isn't an Act of Parlia-
ment," said the young American lady, plaintively
and patiently.   "Why should you regulate all
your movements by her?   You are always looking to the north—you are like the spires of the
churches that are said to be always telling us
that heaven is close by the Pole Star."

"The information is inaccurate, my dear,"
Ingram said, looking at his pipe, "for the spires
of the churches on the other side of the world
point the other way.   However, that does not
matter.   How do you propose rampaging all
over Scotland, and still be at Oban on the
fifteenth?"

"Telegraph to Mr. and Mrs. Lavender to
come on to Edinburgh, and leave the trip to
Lewis until we have seen those places.   For
once we have got to that wild island, who knows
when we shall return? Now do, like a good boy.
You know this new house of theirs will be all
the drier in a month's time.   And their yacht
will be all the more ship-shape.   And both Sheila

and her husband will be the better of coming
down among civilized folks for a few weeks' time
—especially just now, when numbers of their
friends must be in the Highlands—and of course
you get better attention at the hotels when the
season is going on, and they have every preparation
made—and I am told the heather and fern on
the hills look very fine in August—and I am
sure Mr. and Mrs. Lavender will enjoy it very
much, if we get a carriage somewhere and leave
the railways altogether, and drive by ourselves
all through the prettiest districts."

She wished to see the effect of her eloquence
on him. It was peculiar. He put his pipe down
and gravely repeated these lines, with which she
was abundantly familiar—

> *" Sez Vather to I, ' Jack, rin arter him du ! '*
> *Sez I to Vather,' ' I'm darned if I du ! ' "*

" You won't ? " she said.

" The proposal comes too late. How can you
expect Sheila to leave her new house, and that
boy of hers that occupies three-fourths of her
letters, just at this time ? I think it was very
kind of her, mind you, to come away down to
Oban to meet us ; and Lavender too, is giving
up the time out of the best working-season of
the year. Bless you, you will see far more

beautiful things as we go from Oban to Lewis than any you have mentioned. For we shall probably cut down by Scarba and Jura before going up to Skye; and then you will see the coast that you admired so much in Lavender's pictures."

"Is the yacht a large one, Edward?" his wife asked, somewhat timidly.

"Oh, big enough to take our party, a dozen times over."

"Will she tumble about much, do you think?"

"I don't know," Ingram said, with an unkindly grin. "But as you are a weak vessel, Lavender will watch the weather for you, and give it you as smooth as possible. Besides, look at the cleanliness and comfort of a smart yacht! You are thinking of one of those Channel steamers, with their engines and oil."

"Let us hope for the best," said his wife, with a sigh.

They not only hoped for it, but got it. When they left the Crinan and got on board the big steamer that was to take them up to Oban, all around them lay a sea of soft and shining blue, scarcely marred by a ripple. Here and there sharp crags that rose out of the luminous plain seemed almost black; but the farther islands lay soft and hazy in the heat, with the beautiful colours of August tinting the great masses of rock. As they steamed northward through the shining sea, new islands and new channels appeared until they came in sight of the open Atlantic, and that, too, was as calm and as still as a summer night. There was no white cloud in the blue vault of the sky ; there was no crisp curl of a wave on the blue plain of the sea ; but everywhere a clear, radiant, salt-smelling atmosphere, the drowsy haze of which was only visible when you looked at the distant islands, and saw the fine and pearly veil of heat that was drawn over the soft colours of the hills. The sea-birds dipped and disappeared as the big boat churned its way onward. A white solan, far away by the shores of Mull, struck the water as he dived and sent a jet of spray into the air. Colonsay and Oronsay became as faint clouds on the southern horizon ; the jagged coast of Lorne drew near. And then they went up through the Sound of Kerrara, and steamed into the broad and beautiful bay of Oban, and behold ! here was Sheila on the pier, already waving a handkerchief to them, while her husband held her arm, lest in her excitement she should g too near the edge of the quay.

"And where is the boat that we have heard

so much of ? " said Mrs. Kavanagh, when all the kissing and hand-shaking was over.

" There ! " said Sheila, not without some shame-faced pride, pointing to a shapely schooner that lay out in the bay, with her white decks and tall spars shining in the afternoon sun.

" And what do you call her ? " asked Mrs. Kavanagh's daughter.

" We call her *Princess Sheila*," said Lavender. " What do you think of the name ? "

" You couldn't have got a better," Ingram said, sententiously, and interposing as if it was not within his wife's province to form an opinion of any sort. " And where is your father, Sheila ? In Borva ? "

" Oh no, he is here," the girl said, with a smile. " But the truth is, he has driven away to see some gentlemen he knows, to ask if he can have some grouse for you. He should have been back by this time."

" I would not hurry him, Sheila," Ingram said, gravely. " He could not have gone on a more admirable errand. We must await his return with composure. In the meantime, Lavender, do make your fellows stop that man : he is taking away my wife's trunk to some hotel or other."

The business of getting the luggage on board

the yacht was entrusted to a couple of men whom Lavender left on shore; whereupon the newly-arrived travellers put off in a little pinnace and were conveyed to the side of the handsome schooner. When they were on board, an eager exploration followed; and if Sheila could only have undertaken to vouch for the smoothness of the weather for the next month, Mrs. Ingram was ready to declare that at last she had discovered the most charming, and beautiful, and picturesque fashion of living known to civilized man. She was delighted with the little elegancies of the state-rooms; she was delighted with the paintings on the under sky-lights, which had been done by Lavender's own hand; she was delighted with the whiteness of the decks and the height of the tapering spars; and she had no words for her admiration of the beautiful sweep of the bay, the striking ruins of the old castle at the point, the rugged hills rising behind the white houses, and out there in the west, the noble panorama of mountain, and island, and sea.

"I am afraid, Mrs. Ingram," Lavender said, "you will have cause to know Oban before we leave it. There is not a breath of wind to take us out of the bay."

"I am content," she said, with a gracious calm.

"But we must get you up to Borva somehow. There it would not matter how long you were becalmed; for there is plenty to see about the island. But this is a trifle commonplace, you know."

"I don't think so at all. I am delighted with the place," she said. "And so are you, Edward."

Ingram laughed. He knew she was daring him to contradict her. He proposed he should go ashore and buy a few lines with which they might fish for young saithe or lythe over the side of the yacht; but this project was stopped by the appearance of the King of Borva, who bore triumphant proof of the success of his mission in a brace of grouse held up in each hand as a small boat brought him out to the yacht.

"And I was seeing Mr. Hutcheson," Mackenzie said to Lavender, as he stepped on board, "and he is a ferry good-natured man whatever, and he says if there is no wind at all he will let one of his steamers take the yacht up to Loch Sunart, and if there is a breeze at all we will get it there."

"But why should we go in quest of a breeze?" Mrs. Ingram said, petulantly.

"Why, mem," said Mackenzie, taking the matter seriously, "you wass not thinking we could sail a boat without wind ? But I am not sure that there will not be a breeze before night."

Mackenzie was right. As the evening wore on, and the sun drooped in the west, the aspect of affairs changed somewhat, and there was now and again a sort of shiver apparent on the surface of the lake-like bay. When, indeed, the people on board came up on deck just before dinner, they found a rather thunderous-looking sunset spreading over the sky. Into the clear saffron glory of the western sky some dark and massive purple clouds had risen. The mountains of Mull had grown light and milk-like ; and yet they seemed near. The glass-like bay began to move ; and the black shadow f a ship that lay on the gleaming yellow plain began to tremble, as the water cut lines of light across the reflection of the masts. You could hear voices afar off. Under the ruins of the castle, and along the curves of the coast, the shadows of the water were a pure green ; and the rocks were growing still more sharp and distinct in the gathering dusk. There was a cold smell of the sea in the air. And then swiftly the pale colours of the west waxed lurid and fierce ; the mountains became of a glowing purple ; and then all the plain of the sea was dashed with a wild glare

of crimson, while the walls of Dunolly grew
black, and overhead the first scouts of the mar-
shalling forces of the clouds came up in flying
shreds of gold and fire.

"Oh aye, we may hef a breeze the night,"
Mackenzie said.

"I hope we shan't have a storm," Mrs. Ingram
said.

"A storm?   Oh no, no storm at all.   It will
be a ferry good thing if the wind lasts till the
morning."

Mackenzie was not at all sure that there
would be storm enough; and went down to
dinner with the others rather grumbling over the
fineness of the weather.   Indeed, when they
came on deck again, later on in the night, even
the slight breeze that he had hoped for seemed impossible.   The night was perfectly still.   A few
stars had come out overhead, and their light
scarcely trembled on the smooth waters of the
bay.   A cold, fresh scent of seaweed was about,
but no wind.   The orange lights in Oban
burned pale and clear; the red and green lamps
of the steamers and yachts in the bay did not
move.   And when Mrs. Ingram came up to take
Sheila forward to the bow of the boat, to sit
down there, and have a confidential talk with
her, a clear and golden moon was rising over the

sharp black ridge of Kerrara into the still and beautiful skies, and there was not a ripple of the water along the sides of the yacht to break the wonderful silence of the night.

" My dear," she said, " you have a beautiful place to live in."

" But we do not live here," Sheila said, with a smile. " This is to me as far away from home as England can be to you, when you think of America. When I came here the first time I thought I had got into another world, and that I should never be able to get back again to the Lewis."

" And is the island you live in more beautiful than this place ? " she asked, looking round on the calm sea, the lambent skies, and the far mountains beyond, which were grey and ghost-like in the pale glow of the moon.

" If you see our island on such a night as this, you will say it is the most beautiful place in the world. It is the winter-time that is bad, when we have rain and mist for weeks together. But after this year I think we shall spend all the winters in London ; although my husband does not like to give up the shooting and the boating, and that is very good amusement for him when he is tired with his work."

" That island life certainly seems to agree with

him," said Mrs. Ingram, not daring even to hint that there was any further improvement in Sheila's husband than that of mere health; " I have never seen him look so well and strong. I scarcely recognized him on the pier—he was so brown and—and I think his sailor-clothes suit him so well. They are a little rough you know —indeed, I have been wondering whether you made them yourself."

Sheila laughed.

" I have seen you look at them. No, I did not make them. But the cloth, that was made on the island, and it is very good cloth whatever."

" You see what a bad imitation of your costume I am compelled to wear. Edward would have it, you know. I think he'd like me to speak like you, if I could manage it."

" Oh no, I am sure he would not like that," Sheila said, " for many a time he used to correct me, and when he first came to the island I was very much ashamed, and sometimes angry with him——"

" But I suppose you got accustomed to his putting everybody right?" said Mr. Ingram's wife, with a smile.

" He was always a very good friend to me," Sheila said, simply.

" Yes, and I think he is now," said her companion, taking the girl's hand, and forcing herself to say something of that which lay at her
heart, and which had been struggling for utter-
ance during all this beating about the bush.
" I am sure you could not have a better friend
than he is, and if you only knew how pleased we
both are to find you so well—and so happy——"

Sheila saw the great embarrassment in her
companion's face, and she knew the good feeling
that had driven her to this stammering confession.

" It is very kind of you," Sheila said, gently.
" I am very happy—yes—I do not think I have
anything more to wish for in the world."

There was no embarrassment in her manner as
she made this simple avowal; her face was
clear and calm in the moonlight, and her eyes
were looking somewhat distantly at the sea and
the island near. Her husband came forward
with a light shawl, and put it round her shoulders. She took his hand, and for a moment
pressed it to her lips. Then he went back to
where Ingram and old Mackenzie were smoking;
and the two women were left to their confi-
dences. Mrs. Kavanagh had gone below.

What was this great noise next morning, of
the rattling of chains and the flapping of

canvas overhead? There was a slight motion in the boat and a plashing of water around her sides. Was the *Princess Sheila* getting under weigh?

The various noises ceased; so also did the rolling of the vessel, and apparently all was silent and motionless again. But when the ladies had dressed, and got upon deck, behold they were in a new world! All around them were the blue waters of Loch Linnhe, lit up by the brilliant sunshine of the morning. A light breeze was just filling the great white sails; and the yacht, heeling over slightly, was cutting her placid way through the lapping waves. How keen was the fresh smell of the air! Sea-gulls were swooping down and around the tall masts: over there the green island of Lismore lay bright in the sunshine; the lonely hills of Morven and the mountains of Mull had a thousand shades of colour glowing on their massive shoulders and slopes; the ruins of Duart Castle, out at the point, seemed too fair and picturesque to be associated with dark legends of blood. Were these faint specks in the south the far islands of Colonsay and Oronsay? Lavender brought his glass to Mrs. Ingram, and, with many apologies to all the ladies for having woke them up so soon, bade her watch the flight of two herons making in for the mouth of Loch Etive.

They had postponed for the present that southward trip to Jura. The glass was still rising; and the appearance of the weather rendered it doubtful whether they might have wind enough to make such a cruise anything but tedious. They had taken advantage of this light breeze in the morning to weigh anchor and stand across for the Sound of Mull; if it held out, they would at least reach Tobermony, and take their last look at a town before rounding Ardnamurchan and making for the wild solitudes of Skye.

"Well, Cis," Ingram said to his wife, as he busied himself with a certain long fishing line, "what do you think of the Western Highlands?"

"Why did you not tell me of these places before?" she said, rather absently; for the mere height of the mountains along the Sound of Mull—the soft green woods leading up to the great bare shoulders of purple, and grey, and brown above—seemed to draw away one's eyes and thoughts from surrounding objects.

"I have, often. But what is the use of telling?"

"It is the most wonderful place I have ever seen," she said. "It is so beautiful and so desolate at the same time. What lovely colours there are everywhere, on the sea, and on the shores there, and up the hills ; and everything is so bright and gleaming. But no one seems to live here. I suppose you couldn't. The loneliness of the mountains and the sea would kill you."

" My dear child, these are town-bred fancies," he said, in his usual calm and carelessly sententious manner ; " if you lived there, you would have plenty to do besides looking at the hills and the sea. You would be glad of a fine day to let you go out and get some fish, or go up the hills and get some black-cock for your dinner; and you would not get sad by looking at fine colours, as town-folks do. Do you think Lavender and Sheila spend their time in mooning up in that island of theirs?—and that, I can tell you, is a trifle more remote and wild than this is. They've got their work to do ; and when that is done they feel comfortable and secure in a well-built house, and fairly pleased with themselves that they have earned some rest and amusement. I daresay, if you built a cottage over there, and did nothing but look at the sea and the hills, and the sky at night, you would very soon drown yourself. I suppose if a man were to give himself up for three months to thinking of the first formation of the world,

and the condition of affairs before that happened, and the puzzle about how the materials
ever came to be there, he would grow mad.
But few people luckily have the chance of
trying. They've got their bread to earn; if
they haven't, they're bent on killing something
or other—foxes, grouse, deer, and what not—
and they don't bother about the stars, or what
lies just outside the region of the stars. When
I find myself getting miserable about the size
of a mountain, or the question as to how and
when it came there, I know that it is time to
eat something. I think breakfast is ready, Cis.
Do you think you have nerve to cut this hook
out of my finger? and then we can go below."

She gave a little scream, and started up.
Two drops of blood had fallen on Lavender's
white decks.

"No, I see you can't," he said. "Open this
knife, and I will dig it out myself. Bless the
girl, are you going to faint because I have
scratched my finger?"

Lavender, however, had to be called in to
help; and, while the surgical operation was
going forward, Mrs. Ingram said—

"You see we have got town's-folks' hands as
yet. I suppose they will get to be leather by
and by. I am sure I don't know how Mrs.

Lavender can do those things about a boat with the tiny little hands she has."

"Yes, Sheila has small hands, hasn't she?" Lavender said, as he bound up his friend's finger, "but then she makes up for that by the bigness of heart."

It was a pretty and kindly speech, and it pleased Mrs. Ingram, though Sheila did not hear it. Then, when the doctoring was over, they all went below for breakfast, and an odour of fish, and ham, and eggs, and coffee, prevailed throughout the yacht.

"I have quite fallen in love with this manner of life," Mrs. Ingram said. "But, tell me, is it always as pleasant as this? Do you always have those blue seas around you, and green shores? Are the sails always white in the sunlight?"

There was a dead silence.

"Well, I would not say," Mackenzie observed, seriously, as no one else would take up the question; "I would not say it is always ferry good weather off this coast—oh no, I would not say that; for if there wass no rain, what would the cattle do, and the streams?— they would not hef a pool left in them. Oh yes, there is rain sometimes; but you cannot always be sailing about, and when there will be

rain, you will hef your things to attend to indoors. And there is always plenty of good
weather if you wass wanting to tek a trip round
the islands, or down to Oban—oh yes, there is
no fear of that; and it will be a ferry good coast
whatever for the harbour, and there is always
some place you can put into, if it wass coming on
rough, only you must know the coast, and the
lie of the islands, and the rocks about the har-
bours. And you would learn it very soon.
There is Sheila there; there is no one in the
Lewis will know more of the channels in Loch
Roag than she does—not one, I can say that;
and when you go further away, then you must
tek some one with you who wass well acquaint
with the coast. If you wass thinking of having
a yacht, Mr. Ingram, there is one I hef heard of
just now in Rothesay that is for sale, and she
is a ferry good boat, but not so big as this
one——"

"I think we'll wait till my wife knows more
about it, Mr. Mackenzie," Ingram said. "Wait
till she gets round Ardnamurchan, and has
crossed the Minch, and has got the final Atlantic
swell as you run in to Borvabost."

"Edward, you frighten me," his wife said;
"I was beginning to give myself courage."

"But it is mere nonsense!" cried Mackenzie.

impatiently. " Kott pless me! There is no chance of your being ill in this fine weather; and if you had a boat of your own, you would ferry soon get accustomed to the weather—oh, very soon indeed—and you would hef no more fear of the water than Sheila has."

" Sheila has far too little fear of the water," her husband said.

" Indeed, and that is true," said her father; " and it is not right that a young lass should go about by herself in a boat——"

" But you know very well, papa, that I never do that now."

" Oh, you do not do it now," grumbled Mackenzie. " No, you do not do it now. But some day you will forget, when there is something to be done, and you will run a great danger, Sheila."

" But she has promised never to go out by herself; haven't you, Sheila?" her husband said.

" I did. I promised that to you. And I have never been out since by myself."

" Well, don't forget, Sheila," said her father, not very sure but that some sudden occasion might tempt the girl to her old deeds of recklessness.

The two American ladies had little to fear,

The Hebrides received them with fair sunshine and smooth seas; and all the day long their occupation was but to watch the wild birds flying from island to island, and mark the gliding by of the beautiful coasts, and listen to the light rushing of the waves as the fresh sea-breeze flew through the rigging. And Sheila was proud to teach them something of the mystery of sailing a small craft, and would give them the tiller sometimes, while her eye, as clear and keen as her father's, kept watch and ward over the shapely vessel that was making for the northern seas. One evening she said to her friends—

" Do you see that point that runs out on this side of the small islands? Round that we enter Loch Roag."

The last pale light of the sun was shining along the houses of Borvabost as the *Princess Sheila* passed. The people there had made out the yacht long ere she came close to land; and Mackenzie knew that twenty eager scouts would fly to tell the news to Scarlett and Duncan, so that ample preparation would be made in the newly-finished house down by the sea. The wind, however, had almost died away; and they were a long time getting into Loch Roag in this clear twilight. They who were making their first visit to Sheila's island sat contentedly enough on deck, however, amazed and bewildered by the beauty of the scene around them. For now the sun had long sunk, but there was a glow all over the heavens, and only in the far east did the yellow stars begin to glimmer over the dark plain of the Loch. Mealasabahl, Suainabahl, Cracabahl, lifted their grand shoulders and peaks into this wondrous sky, and stood dark and clear there, with the silence of the sea around them. As the night came on the yellow stars grew more intense overhead, but the lambent glow in the north did not pale. They entered a small bay. Up there on a plateau of the rocks stood a long, low house, with all its windows gleaming in the dusk. The pinnace was put off from the yacht; in the strange silence of the night the ripples plashed around her prow; her oars struck fire in the water as the men rowed in to the land. And then, as Sheila's guests made their way up to the house, and when they reached the verandah, and turned to look at the sea, and the Loch, and the far mountains opposite, they beheld the clear and golden sickle of the moon rising from behind the black outline of Suainabhal into the soft and violet skies. As the yellow moon rose in the south, a pathway of gold began to tremble on

Loch Roag, and they could see the white curve
of sand around the bay. The air was sweet
with the cold smell of the sea. There was a
murmur of the far Atlantic all around the silent
coast.

It was the old familiar picture that had
charmed the imagination of Sheila's first and
only lover, when as yet she was to him as some
fair and wonderful Princess, living in a lonely
island, and clothed round about with the glamour
of old legends and stories of the sea. Was she
any longer this strange Sea-Princess, with dreams
in her eyes, and the mystery of the night and the
stars written in her beautiful face? Or was she
to him now—what all the world had long ago
perceived her to be—a tender wife, a faithful
companion, and a true and loyal-hearted woman?
Sheila walked quietly into the house; there was
something for her friends to see; and, with a
great pride, and a gentleness, and a gladness,
Scarlett was despatched on a particular errand.
The old King of Borva was still down at the
yacht, looking after the landing of certain small
articles of luggage. Duncan had come forward
to Ingram and said, "And are you ferry well,
sir?" and Mairi, come down from Mackenzie's
house, had done the same. Then there was a
wild squeal of the pipes in the long apartment

where supper was laid—the unearthly gathering-cry of a clan; until Sheila's husband dashed into the place and threatened to throw John into the sea if he did not hold his peace. John was offended, and would probably have gone up the hill-side, and in revenge, played " Mackrimmon shall no more return," only that he knew the irate old King of Borva would, in such a case, literally fulfil the threat that had been lightly uttered by his son-in-law. In another room, where two or three women were together, one of them suddenly took both Sheila's hands in hers, and said, with a look of kindness in her eyes— " My dear, I can believe now what you told me that night at Oban."

And Sheila's heart was too full to make answer.

THE END.

LONDON: R. CLAY, SONS, AND TAYLOR, PRINTERS.